Promises Kept

Zoe Burton

Promises Kept

Zoe Burton

Published by Sweet Escapes Press

Regular Print Version © 2015 Zoe Burton

Large Print Version © 2022 Zoe Burton

Early drafts of this story were written and posted serially in July 2015 on Jane Austen Fan Fiction forums.

ISBN: 978-1-953138-26-2

Acknowledgements

First, I thank Jesus Christ, my Savior and Guide, without whom this story would not have been told. I love you!

Additional thanks go to my betas, Rose and Leenie. You stretched me and kept me on the straight and narrow, writing-wise. You rock!!

Next, I cannot express deeply enough my appreciation for the readers, writers, and <gasp!> fans (FANS!!!) in my circle at Facebook for their support, encouragement, and inspiration … and chocolate! You are The Bomb!!

Chapter 1

As Elizabeth sat in the slow-moving carriage, looking out the window at the hustle and bustle of London, her mind was elsewhere. She was thinking back to the ride she shared with her husband yesterday.

~~~***~~~

He had ordered their horses saddled before leaving his dressing room. After rousing her from sleep, he persuaded her to go with him. They broke their fasts, then rode to the outskirts of the city, to a large empty field. To her surprise, there was a track worn into the grass all around the edge. She was further surprised to be challenged by her husband to a race. Never one to let such a provocation go unanswered, she
~~~

agreed. Around and around the field they raced, for seven laps. The groom who had accompanied them was pressed into service to count the laps and to wave a handkerchief to signal the end of the contest.

Elizabeth was thrilled with the feeling of the horse moving under her, the thudding of his hooves hitting the ground vibrating up through her bottom, and the air whizzing past her face. Clucking her tongue and tapping him with her riding crop, she urged the horse to go faster and faster, first to catch up to Fitzwilliam, and then to pass him. They ran neck and neck for a while, and at the end, she beat him by just a nose. Exhilarated, she cheered, shrieking her joy in a most unladylike fashion, raising her arms high in the air, then bringing them down to clap loudly. Her husband laughed out loud. Her joy was infectious and he enjoyed seeing it. This was his goal in bringing his beloved wife to this place. He knew that she loved racing her friends and family. She had not had opportunity in a long while to do so.

Bringing her horse around, she trotted him up close beside her husband's. Giving Fitzwilliam a cheeky smile, she leaned over for a kiss.

"Very good, Sweetheart. I did not know you were capable of such a feat," he said to her with a laugh.

"Did you not?" she asked, teasing him in return. "I certainly did. Both my horse and I are so much younger than you; 'twas not a difficult task." She tossed her head as she spoke, raising her nose in the air as she had seen so many high society women do in recent days during her visits. Her words and manner drew another laugh from Fitzwilliam. Drawing his horse to a stop and dismounting, he reached for her, pulling her out of the saddle and into his arms. As the groom, with eyes averted, led the horses away for a further cool-down, Elizabeth's joyous laugh was suddenly stopped by her husband's ardent kiss.

~~~***~~~

Elizabeth's companions in the carriage, her Aunt Gardiner and Lady Matlock, looked at her smile then at each other. It was obvious that their niece was present only physically. Mentally she was somewhere else entirely.

Cocking her eyebrow and nodding to Elizabeth, the lady silently asked a question. With a shrug, Madelyn Gardiner tipped her head in acquiescence. Clearing her throat, she directed a question to Elizabeth.

"Lizzy?"

No response. She tried again, this time a little louder.
~~~

"Lizzy?"

Nothing. Seeing Lady Matlock covering a smile with her hand, Mrs. Gardiner rolled her eyes before trying another time a little more loudly, this time adding in a quick nudge with her elbow.

"Elizabeth!"

Elizabeth jumped, startled out of her daydream. Her hand to her chest, she cried, "What?" After having jumped a bit themselves, her aunts sputtered before dissolving into laughter. Soon they had laughed so hard, tears were running down their faces.

The object of their amusement was rather offended at first. They were laughing at her, and she did not know why. However, her natural tendency toward humor and the infectiousness of their merriment soon overtook her, and she joined in.

As they began to calm, Mrs. Gardiner inquired, "What were you thinking about, Lizzy? I called and called to you, and you never heard me."

Elizabeth smiled as a blush stole over her cheeks. "I was thinking about the race Fitzwilliam and I had yesterday."

"Race? What kind of race?"

"After we broke our fast, he invited me for a ride out to the edge of town. There is a nice large field there, about an acre and a half in size, I believe he said. There is a track worn around the outside of it, and he dared me to race him. You know, Aunt Maddie, how I respond to challenges."

Mrs. Gardiner laughed, "Oh, yes, I do! Please, I am all curiosity now; continue."

With a smile, Elizabeth did so. "There is not much left to tell. We completed several laps, and our groom started us and kept track of the circuits we made, then waved a handkerchief to indicate the end. It was so very enjoyable! I loved the feel of the wind and the pounding of the hooves of my horse vibrating up through the saddle. I have not felt so free, or so … self-assured in a long time!" She leaned forward, an eager smile on her face, her eyes brighter than they had been in weeks, and it was clear to her listeners how enthralled she was with the experience.

Lady Matlock was worried. "But, Elizabeth, it is so dangerous! A lady's stirrup has no hold for your foot! You could have fallen and been injured or killed!"

"Oh, no, Aunt Audra; Fitzwilliam had my stirrups switched to the regular iron ones like his. He said that sidesaddles are dangerous enough, and he does not want to be constantly worrying about me when I'm riding. I know it's not terribly fash-ionable yet, but I have seen other ladies using them. Please do not worry."

"Very well, then. I know that Fitzwilliam is delib-erate in everything he does. I will trust his judgement in this." Lady Matlock turned teasing, asking, "Just who won this contest?"

"Why, I did, my lady," Elizabeth replied with a saucy smile and a wink, causing the three to once more collapse into gales of laughter.

A short while later the carriage stopped in front of their destination — the modiste, who was making Elizabeth some gowns to outfit her for not only the events she would be attending in town, but also some to wear while at Pemberley for the summer. Disembarking the carriage with assistance from the footman, the three ladies quickly entered the shop as the remaining grooms and footmen who had attended them took up places outside the door. Ever since Lord Regis had attacked her at the bookshop, Elizabeth went nowhere without a guard.

Lord Regis was a peer and a member of the House of Lords who had met and tried to court Elizabeth near her father's estate of Longbourn in Hertfordshire. When she refused him, he attempted to force the issue, with her mother's sanction. To keep her safe after the man struck her, she was sent by her father to London to stay with the Gardiners. Regis followed her there, and as a result, her uncle and his friend George Darcy betrothed Elizabeth to Darcy's son, Fitzwilliam. The two married a few days later, following an incident where Regis broke into the Gardiners' house in an attempt to kidnap her.

A couple weeks after the marriage, the newly-wedded Darcys went shopping with George Darcy and the Matlocks. The ladies were waiting in a bookstore for their gentlemen when Elizabeth was once again accosted by the peer. This time, he was stopped by her husband and warned off by her father-in-law. Elizabeth's confidence had been greatly shaken by the initial attack upon her; the second one diminished it further. Fitzwilliam now insisted that she have a guard wherever she went, especially if she was out with other ladies. It was a testament to her low spirits that she did not balk at this at all.

Inside the modiste's establishment, the ladies greeted the proprietress, Madame Claire, who quickly led them to a private room. Once there, Elizabeth sat in a chair with a resigned sigh. She did not enjoy shopping, unless it was for books, and this day looked to be a long one. She despised the endless in and out of gowns in various stages of construction, as well as the poking from the pins and the standing in one spot for hours. She did not understand why she had to be fit for every dress. "They have my measurements, why not just use them and save me the torture?" was a sentiment often heard by her relatives when it was suggested she might want a new outfit or two.

Despite her dislike of the activity, Elizabeth made it through the experience with a minimum of impatience. It helped that Mrs. Gardiner kept everyone in the room entertained with stories of the pranks and problems her niece had fallen into as a child. The abundance of laughter had made the time pass more quickly than it usually did.

"Oh, Mrs. Gardiner," gasped Lady Matlock after a long bout of hilarity, "I can just see it happening! Her poor mother!"

"Yes," Elizabeth laughed, "it is no wonder her nerves are so strained, as she will tell you herself."

At long last, the appointment over and Elizabeth dressed again in the clothes she had been wearing upon entering the shop, the three decided to go to a nearby tea shop. The bookshop had been suggested as their next destination, but was decided against due to Elizabeth's unease. Following tea, the ladies went to their respective homes for a rest.

<center>~~~***~~~</center>

After changing her clothes, lying down for a while, and partaking of some tea and biscuits, Elizabeth was ready to continue her day. It was not difficult for her to relax at Darcy House. She felt the safest there of any other place she knew. She had spent months being anxious, and hated the person she had become as a result of her fear of another attack. She remembered with fondness the feeling of confidence she had a year ago, the feeling that she could conquer the world, or at least her little part of it. She had never before experienced violence. Her parents never hit her. She and her sisters had pulled each other's hair a few times as small children but had been swiftly disciplined and did not continue the practice. She despised the fearfulness that gripped her. She longed for her previous confidence to return. When she had spoken of it to Fitzwilliam, he had assured her that it would come back in time. She could only trust that he was correct.

Taking a few minutes to walk up to the nursery and greet Georgiana helped to redirect Elizabeth's thoughts in a more pleasant direction. After questioning her sister about her lessons and chatting with the governess for a few minutes, she was ready to continue her day.

She headed down the stairs to the drawing room to await her new relatives, Lady Matlock and Viscountess Tansley, who were coming to help her practice her curtsey before the queen. She had already spent many hours each day in the last several weeks rehearsing her entrance to and exit from the royal drawing room. With a tablecloth pinned to her gown to imitate the long train that was part of her court attire, she repeatedly entered the room, curtseyed low before Lady Matlock, who was representing the monarch, and then swept her "train" up with her arm before backing out. Even with all of the walking Elizabeth had done over the course of her life, her legs were tired and sore from all the dipping down and standing back up. However, her performance must be flawless, and the only way to achieve that was to practice constantly, so practice she would.

Rising from the deep curtsey for what seemed the thousandth time that afternoon, she groaned. Her legs felt like they were on fire. Just at that moment, her husband walked in the room.

Fitzwilliam and his father had just arrived home from a meeting with their solicitor, and he immediately went searching for his wife. He was in desperate need of a kiss after several hours discussing investments. Hearing her groan, he strode to her side, anxious to discover what was wrong.

"Elizabeth! Are you well?"

"Darling, you are home!" She was overjoyed to see him. "I am well; it is just that my legs ache from all the curtseys I have been doing." She tipped her face up for a kiss as he drew near, wrapping her arms around his waist as he wrapped his around her. "I have no need to walk for exercise as long as I continue to practice this way," she added.

With a frown on his face and a deep crease between his brows, Fitzwilliam searched her eyes for the truth. "You are certain you are well?"

Elizabeth laughed. "Is that a question or a command?"

His brow clearing a bit and his lips curving into a small smile, he replied, "Perhaps it is a little of both. I cannot bear the thought of you being unwell in any form."

Addressing Lady Matlock, he inquired of her, "Aunt, has she not had enough for today? She has practiced daily for weeks now, and it is obvious to me that she is in pain from it. Can she not stop now and rest her legs? She can continue to practice on the morrow or even the day after."

"Fitzwilliam, you well know that her curtsey must

be perfect, and the only way to achieve that perfection is to constantly practice, over and over again. Surely you have heard your Aunt Catherine say the very same thing?"

It was now Fitzwilliam's turn to groan. "Yes, Aunt Audra, I have. Every time I have seen her, I have heard it repeated ad nauseam."

Laughing, Lady Matlock replied with a wink, "Well, then, surely you know your wife must also practice."

Eventually, though, the countess was convinced that her newest niece had endured enough for the day. The ladies unpinned Elizabeth's tablecloth and took places on the sofas as they waited for the housekeeper to bring tea things and for Fitzwilliam to fetch his father.

"You are doing very well, Elizabeth, with your

curtsey," the viscountess stated. "I am certain you will be well prepared to be presented. How goes the progress on your gown?"

"It goes very well. Madame Claire was here yesterday for a final fitting, as I had not expected to go out again. Then my aunts invited me shopping today, and when I saw her this morning, she promised to have it here on the morrow. If I am performing as well as you say I am with the curtsey, I should be well-prepared for the event."

Elizabeth and her guests paused in their conversation as, simultaneously, Fitzwilliam and his father entered the room and the tea was brought in and laid out for her to pour. Observing the housekeeper pulling the door shut behind her, Lady Matlock began to speak.

"Yes, you will do well, I am convinced." The lady paused, and then coming to a decision, acted upon it by continuing quietly, "Are you nervous? I have seen how quiet you become in unfamiliar company. Fitzwilliam and his father have told you, have they not, of the steps they have taken to protect you?"

At Elizabeth's nod, the countess sniffed, adding, "Not that they will be necessary. He is a coward, Regis is; he has been frightened away, never to return. Why, the earl himself told me the man has not been seen in any of the most popular places since …" She glanced at her niece. "That day. Do not waste your time on fear of him, my dear. You have your guards and all the Darcy and Fitzwilliam men to protect you."

Mr. Darcy and Fitzwilliam nodded at her words, Fitzwilliam taking his wife's hand.

Looking to her daughter-in-law, Lady Matlock added, "And the Fitzwilliam ladies will never leave you unattended. Is that not correct, Vanessa?"

"Indeed it is. I cannot imagine the horror you faced, to be assaulted in such a way. No woman, especially not a gentlewoman, should be treated in such an infamous manner! We will remain by your side at any time your husband or father-in-law leaves you alone." She reached over with a gentle smile and grasped Elizabeth's free hand, squeezing it lightly. "You are family, and we take care of our own."

Letting go at her cousin's answering smile, Vanessa leaned back and then said, "Let us speak of something more pleasant, shall we? Mother, will you tell Elizabeth what happened when your besotted groom asked that young scullery maid to walk the park with him? I am sure my cousin would love a laugh right about now; that poor maid was frightened to the bone, I am positive!"

Lady Matlock laughed. "Oh, yes! Oh Elizabeth, it was so amusing …"

And so the remaining time the group was together was spent in delighted laughter.

~~~***~~~

A week later, Elizabeth was presented. She performed her curtsey flawlessly, and she made a good impression on the monarch, who was impressed with the determination and trepidation that appeared at the same time in her eyes.

Backing from the room, she breathed a sigh of relief that it was over, and turned to seek out her husband and his father. Searching the room, she found them striding toward her from the direction of the door.
~~~

When he reached her side, Fitzwilliam took hold of her hand to kiss her fingers. "Well, Sweetheart, how was it? Did you trip as you feared you might?"

"No, I did not. You may stop teasing me now," she retorted, eyebrow rising as she glared at him and his twinkling eyes. "If the smile I received is any indication, I did very well. Aunt Audra drilled me incessantly. I was unable to do anything but perform flawlessly."

Her husband chuckled. "I was never in any doubt. You have been quite determined these past weeks, continuing on when another woman would have given up. I am proud of you, Wife." He tucked her hand in the crook of his elbow before turning his attention to his parent.

"Father, what say you to returning home? Elizabeth's work is done, and if she feels anything akin to me, she would enjoy changing her attire into something more comfortable than court dress."

Laughing, Mr. Darcy replied in the affirmative, and the group slowly made their way out of the palace and on to their home. They would have a few hours to eat, rest, and relax before leaving for Matlock House and the ball that Lady Matlock had planned to celebrate this momentous occasion in her niece's life.

Georgiana was waiting in the foyer for them when they arrived. She was eager to see Elizabeth in her presentation gown, but had been at her lessons when her brother and sister left for court. Her excitement upon seeing them led her to squeal, which then caused her father to remind her that ladies are quiet and children unseen and unheard. The twinkle in his eye gave lie to his words, and caused the governess to sigh to herself and look away so she could roll her eyes.

"Elizabeth! You are so beautiful! Look at that gown!" Georgiana's enthusiasm for the dress put smiles on the faces of those witnessing it. She reached for her sister's hands, holding them out and then urging her to turn around. "Oh, Sister! How lovely!" she sighed. "I hope when I am presented that I can wear a gown like that!"

Laughing, Elizabeth pulled her in for a hug before dryly stating, "You may change your mind once you are actually wearing the thing. It is not altogether easy to maneuver in these hoops."

"Oh, but look at you! Who cares about ease of movement when one can look so grand?" More laughter, this time from all her family, pulled her eyes away from the gown. "What? Am I wrong?

Do you not agree that Lizzy in that dress is perfect?"

"Yes, Sister, she is, but then …" Fitzwilliam looked tenderly at his wife. "To me she always looks perfect."

"Of course," Georgiana replied, rolling her eyes in such an obvious manner that her father had to turn away to hide his guffaw and Elizabeth had to smother a laugh with her hand. "If you were to think otherwise, I would fear you were ill. Really, Fitzwilliam, sometimes I wonder how such an intelligent man can wander about without a single clue about the women around him."

At that, no one could hold in their laughter and hilarity reigned for several minutes. Even her brother had to laugh at the manner in which Georgiana had presented her statement. Eventually, though, she was sent up to the nursery with a mild reprimand for being disrespectful, and the rest went up to their rooms to change clothes and spend some time in quiet pursuits before their evening outing.

Chapter 2

Hours later, Elizabeth was nervous. The ball she was dressing for was her first as a married woman. All the days spent shopping, endless hours standing for fittings with the modiste, countless hours practicing her curtsey, and interminable mornings spent making visits with her new aunt came down to this one night. Of course, she had not yet met all of the most important members of her new society. There had not been time for that. She would make their acquaintance tonight. First impressions were important, and she knew that she must make a good one this night if she wished to be accepted by her husband's peers and to make him proud. She started to wipe her sweaty hands down the beautiful white and purple ball gown and then, suddenly realizing what she was about, stopped and reached instead for a towel that was laying on her dressing table.

Behind her came the sound of a door opening. Glancing in the mirror, she saw her husband enter. The young couple shared this dressing room, as well as a sitting room and bed chamber. They had not taken a wedding trip, but had instead spent a week cloistered together in this suite. They had known each other for years before marrying; they spent their wedding week learning about each other on an entirely different level. As a result, they made the decision to keep this chamber as their own.

Elizabeth turned and held her hands out to her Fitzwilliam. "You look quite dashing, my darling," she said with a smile.

Her spouse took her hands as he leaned in to

kiss her cheek, a smile gracing his features. "Thank you."

Leaning away again, he continued, "You, my beloved wife, are the most gorgeous creature I have ever beheld. You will outshine every woman in the room tonight. I am blessed to be the man escorting you."

Elizabeth blushed. "You are quite the charmer when you wish to be! I will be happy if no one else notices me, to be honest." She breathed in deeply, letting it out in a sigh.

She looked earnestly up at his face. "I want you to be proud of me; but I am anxious about the gentlemen that will be in attendance."

Fitzwilliam knew that what she was really asking for was reassurance that Lord Regis was not going to be there. His father had warned the man off, but Regis was sly, and as a result, their investigator had men following him at all times.

Holding her close again, Fitzwilliam laid his cheek on the top of her head and reassured her, "Do not worry, Sweetheart. Remember, Lord Regis is being watched and has to this point not emerged from his home except for attending to his duties as a legislator. Father has ordered extra footmen to ride on the carriage, and has armed them, and he hired guards to watch the entrances of Matlock House. If the man was to attempt anything, and I do not believe that he will, he would not be successful. I promised to protect you, and I will." Giving her a squeeze, he asked, "Do you trust me?"

Elizabeth tightened her hold on his middle. "Yes, Fitzwilliam, I do trust you." Smiling up at him from her position cradled in his arms, she softly said, "I love you."

Her husband could not resist her when she was so close and smiling at him. He groaned quietly and bent his head to kiss her thoroughly. A few minutes later, after reassuring her of his equally ardent feelings, he let go of her, drew her arm up under his, and escorted her out of the room and down the stairs.

~~~***~~~

Matlock House was situated only a couple streets away from Darcy House. On a fine day, it was a short walk, and the families often chose to travel the distance in that manner. However, at night and in ball attire, this was not a possibility, and so the Darcys boarded their carriage and were soon disembarking at their destination. Being the guests of honor, they were the first to arrive, thus avoiding the crippling traffic that would soon clog the lane. Their hosts greeted them in the foyer.
~~~

"Elizabeth," Lady Matlock exclaimed, grabbing hold of her hands as soon as the maid had taken her cloak and bonnet. "You look stunning! I knew when I saw the drawing that this was the dress for you." She leaned in and kissed her niece's cheek. "How are you feeling? You are not frightened, are you? You know we would let nothing happen to you here."

"I know you would not." Elizabeth sighed. "I used to say that my courage rose with every attempt to intimidate me, but right now that courage is sadly lacking. However, I have my Fitzwilliam by my side along with you and the rest of my new family. I know all will be well. I promise that I will not let anyone know of my unease."

Squeezing the hands she still held, Lady Matlock smiled. "I know you will not, my dear. I have every confidence in you," she stated as she released

Elizabeth and turned to her brother and nephew. "You have taken the steps Henry spoke to you about, have you not?"

Lord Matlock answered, "Yes, my dear; George and I interviewed the guards and extra footmen together. All is in place to guarantee the safety of everyone in attendance tonight."

"Good. Come then, I hear a carriage pulling up. We must receive our guests." And so saying, she lined the five of them up and turned toward the door.

Elizabeth looked up at her husband just as he glanced down. He saw the uneasy smile on her face and squeezed the hand on his arm and winked at her. Feeling her relax as her smile grew larger and more serene, he turned back toward the approaching guests.

First to arrive were Elizabeth's aunt, uncle, and eldest sister. She greeted them with hugs and kisses, smiling in relief that the family members she was closest to were the first attendees she should see.

"Jane, you are lovely, as always. If fully half of the men here tonight are not in love with you before the event is ended, I shall be surprised!"

"Oh, Lizzy! How silly you are! I shall be well pleased just to have a few dances. I wish to marry for love, as you seem to have done." She winked at her sister, glancing at Fitzwilliam, who could not keep his eyes off his wife. "Brother, is she not very well-turned-out this evening?"

Fitzwilliam startled at being addressed. He smiled, then squeezed Elizabeth's hand on his arm before replying, "Indeed, Sister, she is very beautiful. Quite the handsomest woman I have seen in a long time."

"Stop, the two of you." Elizabeth laughed. "You shall turn my head, and I shall become insufferable."

"Oh, we would never allow that, Sweetheart."

The three laughed, along with the Gardiners, who had listened to the entire conversation with delight at the happiness they saw on Elizabeth's face. They would have liked to continue in this manner; however, more guests had arrived.

"Jane, let us move along. Lizzy, Fitzwilliam, we will speak again later."

"Thank you, Uncle Edward." Elizabeth squeezed his hand as he moved past her before turning to smile at the new person to whom she was being introduced.

~~~***~~~

An hour later, she sagged against her husband as the last guest turned and proceeded to the ballroom.
~~~

"Oh, my! That was certainly momentous! I have never greeted so many people at one time in my life," she said with a laugh.

"You did very well, my dear," Lady Matlock assured her. Turning to her husband, she continued, "Well, my lord, shall we begin the dancing?"

With a twinkle in his eye, he held out his arm for his wife and replied, "Yes, I believe we shall." He moved them in the direction of the ballroom.

Fitzwilliam had by this time wrapped Elizabeth in his arms. "We will follow directly, Papa," he informed his parent as he rubbed his wife's back.

Mr. Darcy smiled. "Do not be too long. We cannot start the dancing without the guests of honor."

With that, he followed the Matlocks into the ballroom.

Elizabeth giggled and looked up with a smile.

Her Fitzwilliam, who had been watching his father walk down the hallway, looked down at her and winked before leaning down for a tender kiss. Too soon to please either, they broke away from each other, glancing regretfully down the hall. After making sure they were still presentable, they followed their family to the ballroom and made their way to the head of the line. Taking their places between the Matlocks on the left and another married couple on the right, the two looked at each other and quickly became lost to everything happening around them. They were caught unaware when the dance began, quickly catching their places in the movements with blushes spreading over their faces. When they moved close enough to speak, Fitzwilliam leaned toward her and said, "You do realize this is our first dance?"

Elizabeth caught her breath. He was correct! They had never even practiced together before.

This was the very first time the two of them had danced. She smiled her delight. The remainder of that set was enchanting. They performed as one, their movements matching perfectly. When the dance brought them together, they flirted shamelessly; and when it pulled them apart, they sought each other with their eyes, often to the detriment of conversation with anyone else. When it ended and he had bowed and she had curtseyed, they made their way to the refreshment table. Whispers surrounded them.

"Besotted. Utterly besotted, the pair of them!"

"Did you see the way he looked at her? Oh, to have my Robert gaze at me, just once, in that manner!"

"… Mr. Darcy engaged them when they were children."

"No! But Lady Catherine has always said …"

"Really! The way he was fawning over the niece of a tradesman! You would think his father would have raised him better!"

"Ah, but you see, his father is quite friendly with said tradesman. I am not at all surprised to see the match. Why, the families spent every summer together at Pemberley, if I am not mistaken. And I was told …"

Elizabeth leaned close to Fitzwilliam and quietly said, "Well, it would seem the word Lady Matlock and I put out only added fuel to an already raging fire. I heard a variation of it whispered as we walked this way, but some of the other stories … oh my!"

Fitzwilliam chuckled before replying. "Indeed, Sweetheart. It seems we have set high society on its ear. Did you not hear any of this when you and my aunt went on your visits in the last couple of weeks?"

"Well, yes, but we disseminated our own version of events, and I assumed it would be believed and would replace the gossip that already prevailed. It sounds to me as though few have actually heard the tale!"

At this point, they reached the table, Fitzwilliam taking two cups of punch and handing one to his wife before offering his arm to her again and leading her to a pair of seats off to the side of the room, near where the Gardiners were seated. They sat together for a time, chatting with her aunt and uncle, unmolested by the other guests. It was not long, however, before their peace was invaded.

"Mr. Darcy, how good it is to see you here this evening."

Fitzwilliam looked up to see the one person in the room he truly wished to never set eyes on again. He and Elizabeth rose to greet Lady Penelope Mays, a woman he was most uncomfortable with, as she had thrown herself at him in the past.

"Lady Penelope, I believe you have already met my wife, Mrs. Elizabeth Darcy?"

Lady Penelope glanced at Elizabeth, giving an obviously half-hearted and insincere smile and nod in her direction before turning her attention back to her prey. "Indeed, I believe we were introduced in the receiving line. We were all surprised at your marriage. Everyone expected you to marry … differently … than you did."

Fitzwilliam had grown more and more rigid from the moment he recognized who was speaking to them. It was obvious to him, and to Elizabeth, and everyone within hearing range, he imagined, that the lady was cutting his wife. "Indeed," he intoned coldly. "I am sure many people had ideas of what I would do. However, none of those people are in charge of me. It is not for them to have any feelings at all about who I married, or about any other aspect of my life. Mrs. Darcy is perfect for me; she is a lady in every way. She has manners and accomplishments other women can only dream of possessing. She is well-bred and polite, poised and serene. There is much you could learn from her. Good day, madam." With that, he stepped away from Lady Penelope, bringing his wife along, her relatives following. The woman he had spoken to, standing with her mouth hanging open at his words of censure, did not move for many minutes. She stood, alone, collecting her thoughts and the attention of those around her. Finally, she gathered her tattered dignity together and moved to another part of the room.

Lady Penelope Mays was the younger sister of

one of Darcy's classmates at Eton and Cambridge. He had first been introduced to her the year he turned twenty, when he spent six weeks at the Mays' family estate. Her father, Lord Peter Mays, had inherited the Earldom of Sheffield just a few months before Darcy's visit. The brother, one Lord Paul Mays, now Viscount Westerville, had thrown the house party as a way to celebrate his ascension.

From the first sight of her brother's handsome friend, Lady Penelope had been enamored of him. He was tall, with thick, dark hair kept just a little long. He was quiet, but she did not mind that; once they were married, she decided, if he was still quiet, she could find other ways to entertain herself. His best feature, of course, was his wealth. The lack of a title was disappointing, but everyone knew the Darcys owned half of Derbyshire. That money more than made up for any other lack.

During that house party, Lady Penelope had tried to make herself indispensable, to imprint herself on his mind so that when he was ready to take a wife, she would be his first choice. She had even tried to arrange a compromising situation a couple times, but something always occurred to prevent it. While she was frustrated when he left without more than a nod in her direction, she had not become desperate yet, knowing he still had to finish his courses at university before he could marry.

When she read in the papers, mere days after his return from his tour of the Kingdom, of his marriage to some female she had never heard of, Lady Penelope was furious. Her plans for her future were in ruins around her. She had not been appeased at meeting the new Mrs. Darcy. The woman had little beauty, and if rumors were to be believed, little dowry. What he saw in the country nobody was beyond Lady Penelope's comprehension. There was nothing she could do about the marriage, she knew. It was done, and it would take an act of Parliament to undo it.

Now here she stood, in a ballroom, having been censured severely by the object of her matrimonial wishes. If she were a lesser woman, she would have been crushed at the severity of Mr. Fitzwilliam Darcy's words; however, Penelope Mays was the daughter of an earl. She had power, and she knew how to use it. She had decided before the ball to ruin the new Mrs. Darcy in her husband's eyes. The meaningless chit did not deserve her new position, and she intended to make sure the lady was more than aware of it. Nothing would please her more than to make the other woman feel her inferiority, and she was now more determined than ever to do so.

Nodding to herself, she began to pay attention to the conversations around her. Soon she was contributing, dropping little snippets of things here and there about the woman she wanted to bring down.

"She had no dowry, you know."

"None? Whatsoever?"

"Not a penny."

"A fortune hunter? Surely Mr. Darcy would not let his son be so taken in!"

"Oh, but you see, he was, as well …"

Early the next morning, as she left the ball with her parents, Lady Penelope was pleased with what she perceived as her progress. She envisioned the gossip that would spread, and the results, with glee.

However, the lady was not as successful as she had hoped. Those who were intimate friends of the Matlocks and Darcys had already spoken with the families and in many cases had met Elizabeth previously. They were inclined to like the young woman, and to discount Lady Penelope's hints as vitriol spread by a rejected hopeful.

Of course, she had her supporters, some who enjoyed her company, some who disliked her but tolerated her for the connection, and some who were in fear of her censure. Those young ladies and gentlemen accepted her unspoken challenge to spread her words, regardless of their belief in the truth of them.

Lady Penelope had a strong personality, never fearing to express herself. She was the only daughter, the last child following a string of four boys. Spoiled as a child, she grew up very sure of herself and her beliefs. The only difference in her now from the child she was then was that she had become more subtle in her manner of getting her way, and imposing her will on others.

Chapter 3

After leaving Lady Penelope standing alone, Fitzwilliam and Elizabeth strode across the room. Feeling the tension still in her husband's arm, Elizabeth leaned against his shoulder and spoke. "Please stop; I cannot keep up with your long strides."

Immediately coming to a halt, he looked to her and apologized. "I am sorry, Sweetheart. Her attitude made me very angry. I should not have taken it out on you." He lifted her hand to bestow a kiss then set it back on his arm, covering it with his own.

"There is nothing to forgive, my darling. I own to being relieved to be so quickly removed from her presence." Elizabeth smiled a little, covering her mouth to muffle a laugh in response to his slight chuckle.

"I knew already that not everyone would like me, Fitzwilliam. Her slight was not entirely unexpected. I think I remember meeting her brother once at Pemberley, oh, a couple years ago?" She turned to her aunt Gardiner, asking, "Do you remember, Aunt?" At the lady's nod, she turned back to Fitzwilliam and continued, "Her brother is Lord Westerville, is he not?" When her husband murmured his reply, she continued. "I would imagine that Lady Penelope is one of those disappointed ladies described by Aunt Audra and Vanessa?"

Fitzwilliam sighed. "Yes, I believe she is. I remember spending six weeks or so at their estate that summer, before we came to Pemberley and you met him. I recall that she seemed to be everywhere I was, always asking me questions about my preferences and my father's estate. I could not move without tripping over her. It was frustrating; I was never so glad to leave a place in my life!"

Elizabeth's grin was wide. "Poor Fitzwilliam, to be so admired at such a young age."

Shaking his head and chuckling softly, he replied, "Hush, Wife. Do you not know I am your master and not to be teased?"

Rolling her eyes, she laughed at him again, squeezing his arm tightly. Before she could respond, Viscount Tansley approached.

"Elizabeth, I believe the next set belongs to me." He held his arm out to her, then looked at his cousin. "Do not worry, Darcy, she will be safe with me."

"I know; I simply do not enjoy seeing her dance with anyone else. I suppose I must accustom myself to it, as the night is still young, and I am certain she will be asked by many more gentlemen."

Tansley laughed quietly before replying, "Indeed.

We will keep an eye on her, all of us. And she is so besotted with you that she will not notice anyone else in the room; is that not so, Elizabeth?"

"Yes, it is," she responded quietly, gazing at her husband with that soft look he so loved. "I may be dancing with other men, but I am going home with you, my darling." She took hold of the hand that hung limply at his side and squeezed it tightly, rejoicing inside when he squeezed back. "I will return as soon as I am able. Perhaps Vanessa would like a dance?"

Smiling at her, he said, "I will ask her. It would not be a punishment to stand up with her if I cannot have you. I love you."

"I love you."

With that, the viscount led her away to the line of dancers.

Fitzwilliam decided to stay back, visiting with the Gardiners while keeping a close eye on his wife, rather than dance with his cousin. Soon they were joined by his friend, Charles Bingley.

"Bingley! So good to see you! I was not sure you would make it this evening. Let me introduce you to my wife's aunt and uncle. Elizabeth is dancing with Tansley; you can meet her later." He gestured out to the dance floor. "Charles Bingley, may I present Mr. and Mrs. Edward Gardiner of Gracechurch Street? Mr. Gardiner is a friend of my father's and a very successful warehouse owner. My father and I have enjoyed the fruits of some very lucrative investments in his business."

Bingley and Gardiner bowed to each other. "I am very pleased to meet you, Mr. Gardiner, Mrs. Gardiner. My roots are in trade, as well. My father was a watch maker in Yorkshire."

"That is where I have heard the name before! I believe I met your father once or twice. I have done business with him in the past! I was sorry to hear of his passing."

"Thank you; it was a difficult time for the whole family. My mother died not six months later. Father was an excellent man, in all respects."

"Oh, I am so sorry," Mrs. Gardiner replied. "How terrible to lose both so closely together! Were they recent losses?"

"I have just come out of mourning, actually. This is the first event I have attended. I spent the last few months in my hometown, dealing with the disposition of my father's business and seeing to my sisters."

"They did not come with you this evening?"

Fitzwilliam asked. He had been surprised to not see them. Elizabeth had never met any of the Bingleys, and he was not looking forward to her meeting the unmarried sister, another lady who made a nuisance of herself by hanging all over him at every turn.

"No, they did not. Hurst and Louisa were called to his parents' estate to attend some business. Caroline is visiting a friend from school for a few weeks. She wanted to come to town with me, but I felt it was best for her to stay away for a while longer." Bingley was well aware that his sister had set her cap at Darcy; she had not taken the news of his marriage well, and he worried about what she might do were she to meet the new Mrs. Darcy so soon. Hopefully, she would meet someone at the house party she was attending and emerge engaged herself. At the least, he hoped the time away would lessen her irritation.

After a few more minutes of chatting, the set ended, and Elizabeth was returned to her spouse's side. At the same time, Jane, who also had been dancing, arrived on the arm of her partner.

"Are you enjoying yourself, Jane? You have yet to be without a partner," Elizabeth teased.

"I am! Oh, Lizzy, this home is so beautiful, the musicians perform perfectly, and the gentlemen are so … gentlemanly! How could I not have a good time?"

While the two were talking, Bingley was staring, open-mouthed, at the most beautiful creature he had ever beheld. She was speaking to another gorgeous lady, one whose hand had been quickly seized by his friend. He could only assume the dark-haired one was the new Mrs. Darcy. That meant … delight of all delights … the beautiful blonde must be with the Gardiners, which meant she was here alone. Oh, he thought, I must have an introduction!

Fitzwilliam, who had noticed his friend's rapt attention to his newest sister, was laughing to himself. Finally allowing a chuckle to be released, he said, "Bingley, may I introduce you to my wife, Elizabeth, and her sister, Miss Jane Bennet?"

Snapped out of his thoughts by his friend's words, Bingley bowed. "Mrs. Darcy, it is such a delight to meet you! I have heard much of you. Your husband has been singing your praises for a long time, but most especially since your marriage. I have received several letters telling me of his happiness. Thank you for accepting him!"

Elizabeth smiled, delight suffusing her face, as she thanked him. "It was my very great honor, I assure you."

Fitzwilliam cleared his throat, bestowing an adoring look on his wife as Bingley turned to greet Jane. "Miss Bennet, I am honored to meet you."

Curtseying, Jane returned his greeting.

"If you are not otherwise engaged, might I have your next set?"

"I am not engaged, sir, and I would be happy to dance with you."

"Excellent!" Bingley beamed, thrilled to be able to dance with this delightful young woman.

A few more minutes of conversation, and the next dance was about to begin. Mr. Bingley escorted Jane to the floor, and Lieutenant Richard Fitzwilliam, Lord Tansley's younger brother and Elizabeth's husband's other cousin, invited her to dance with him, leading her out, as well.

Jane and Bingley seemed to take to each other

instantly. By the end of their first set together, they were chatting as though they had known each other all their lives. They went on to dance with other partners, but came together again for the supper set. During the meal, they sat as close as they dared, talking only between themselves, unless forced to do otherwise by their amused friends and, in Jane's case, family.

"Tell me about your family, Miss Bennet. Darcy introduced me to your sister, and you have told me there are others. Are they older or younger?"

"They are all younger, sir. Mrs. Darcy is next to me, followed by Mary, then Kitty, and finally Lydia. My youngest sister is eleven. Mrs. Darcy is sixteen, and the other two girls are a year or two apart."

"How delightful! I have only two sisters: Louisa, who is married to a Mr. Hurst, and my twin sister

Caroline, who is unmarried and visiting one of her friends. Your younger sisters, are they as delightful as you and Mrs. Darcy?"

Jane laughed quietly, "My younger sisters are very different than me and Elizabeth. Mary is quiet, though she does like to give advice to those around her. Kitty and Lydia are rather high-spirited. Kitty follows where Lydia leads, though Lydia is younger. I am sure that with a few more years, their high spirits will give way to a more mature manner of behaving, though they are already delightful girls."

Elizabeth leaned over to inject, "What she means, Mr. Bingley, is that our two youngest sisters are spoiled. You will find that Jane sees only the good and none of the bad in those around her."

Jane blushed. "Lizzy!"

"I see nothing wanting in your sister, Mrs. Darcy.

I'm sure she is aware of their faults, just as I am aware of those in my own siblings." He smiled warmly at Jane. "Her outlook matches my own, I believe," he added softly.

Elizabeth smothered a laugh at their besotted expressions before returning to her husband's conversation with his cousin. Jane and Bingley returned to their discourse, as well.

"Tell me more of your family, Mr. Bingley. You said your parents have passed. What were they like?"

"I was not terribly close with either of my parents, unfortunately. My father was a very busy man, always working, expanding his business with the goal of being successful enough that I would be able to become a landed gentleman. He did very well; I hope in the near future to find an estate to lease, with an eye to purchase. I would buy right away, but your new brother tells me I might do better to lease first."

"He is very wise, is he not? Lizzy tells me he shares his thoughts on everything with her; she has been greatly impressed with the depth of consideration he applies to every decision. She says he has learned that from his father."

"Indeed, Mr. Darcy and his son are very much alike, and in more than looks! I am proud to be able to call Fitzwilliam my friend and to be accepted by his father. They are unlike many others of their station, but their acceptance has gone a long way to gaining mine with the same people."

"That is wonderful, Mr. Bingley!"

"Indeed." He smiled at her, wishing he could hold her hand. "Well, now that I have told you about my father, let me tell you about my mother. She was very different than he. My mother had lofty goals. She wanted to be the mistress of the manor, and for my father to be the master. I fear that her desire to rise further than was possible led to strife between them on occasion. It certainly gave my twin high goals."

Here he laughed. "My twin. Mother made sure every year as our birthday approached that we understood just how hard she toiled to bring us into the world, and just how much we owed her in adulation. But we were also her rising stars, and she had great expectations of us. We were not close to her, really. We spent the majority of our time, all three of us, with the governess and tutors or at school. I do remember hearing her boast of our accomplishments, though.

"My parents both died in the last year and six months. Both became ill when a sickness swept through Scarborough, where they lived. My father sickened first; it took him quickly. My mother caught it not long after, but she lingered much longer before death carried her away." He paused, then continued. "As I said before, I was not terribly close to either of them, and they did have moments when I wondered why they had married, but I miss them, and I believe that they loved each other in their own way. I think that if my father had not died, my mother may have survived, as well. But, there is no way of knowing that. We must all move on."

Jane gave him an understanding smile. "That would be very hard. I cannot imagine losing my parents, either of them. I think perhaps my mother and father have a marriage similar to that of yours. My father keeps to his book room, and joins the family but rarely. My mother's joy in life is gossip. Her goal is, I believe, to see each of us married well."

"An admirable goal. Mine desired that for my sisters, as well, I believe. I am glad she was able to see Louisa married before she took ill."

Fitzwilliam intruded into their conversation with a statement to the table. "I hear the musicians tuning up again. Let us join the rest in returning to the ballroom."

Reluctantly, Bingley and Jane parted to dance with still more people. As much as both longed for a third dance, it simply was not done. Neither was willing to upset and embarrass those closest to them in such a manner. They did, however, spend the time between sets together as much as possible, and before the night was over, Mr. Bingley asked and received permission to call on Miss Bennet the next day. The Gardiners were pleased with this. They liked the young man, and hoped that the two would come to an understanding, as Jane's future would then be secured. It did not hurt that she would be spared her mother's anger and despair should she arrive back at Longbourn without a suitor.

Elizabeth danced with several other gentlemen that evening, all vetted by her husband and father-in-law. While she was nervous to the point of quivering, nothing untoward happened, and by the last dance, set aside for Fitzwilliam, she was beginning to calm. Of course, being held so closely by the man she adored did much to put her at peace. She never felt as safe as she did when he held her. As the guests began to leave, Mr. Darcy approached to inform them that he had called for the carriage. Elizabeth farewelled her sister, aunt and uncle and then excused herself to visit the ladies' parlor that had been set aside for their use, knowing the wait for the carriage might be long.

Entering the room alone, as Lady Matlock and the Viscountess were both occupied with other matters and could not accompany her, she saw that it was crowded with ladies doing as she was in preparation for leaving. Finally, as the room began to empty, she was able to take care of her needs before taking time to assess her appearance in the mirror provided for that. As she stood in front of the glass, thinking she must be the last to use it for the night, she was surprised to see two other young women enter, one blonde, one brunette. Seeing her, they approached.

"Well, what have we here?" sneered the blonde.

"Why, don't you know, Cecilia, this is Mrs. Darcy. She is the mouse from the country that forced Mr. Fitzwilliam Darcy into marriage," replied the brunette.

"Indeed, I had heard that." Speaking to Elizabeth, Cecilia said, "What makes you think you will ever fit into our society?" Her voice began to carry a spiteful tone. "You are nothing, and you will never be anything, regardless of who you married. He will come to regret you, and it will not take long."

Suddenly, the woman reached out and yanked the curl dangling over Elizabeth's shoulder hard enough to make her cry out. "You do not belong, do you hear me?" She yanked again, eliciting another yelp of pain from her victim. "I plan to make your life miserable at every chance I get."

The brunette laughed. Seeing Elizabeth's mouth opening to retort, she slapped her. "There is no point in telling anyone about this, Mrs. Darcy. No one will believe you. If anyone notices redness on your face, you will tell them you ran into the door. Do I make myself clear?" When her victim did not respond immediately, she slapped her again. Finally, after seeing Elizabeth nod, the pair laughed and exited the room.

Knowing that her family would soon come looking for her, Elizabeth did her best to soothe the redness left by the slaps. It was not possible to completely eradicate them, but she did hope no one noticed, least of all Fitzwilliam.

She was quiet as she joined her husband and his father in the foyer, accepting her coat and bonnet from the maid. Fitzwilliam looked at her closely, suspicion in his eyes. The remaining guests had already gone home, so she had no reason to be reticent. Perhaps she is tired, he thought. She did not turn to face him at all, and took his left arm instead of the one on the right that he had offered her. The Darcys each wished their hosts a good night, then left the house to enter their carriage for the short ride home.

Sitting beside her in the conveyance, Fitzwilliam was again struck by her silence. He put his arm around her, asking if she was well.

"Yes, I am well," was her quiet response.

"I am not certain of that, Sweetheart. You are far too quiet." He looked across the carriage to his father, but in the darkness could not see him. "We will speak more after we retire to our rooms."

"Very well, Husband." Elizabeth knew that he now had suspicions that something happened while she was away from his side. She would do her best to put him off so she had time to think about what occurred, but knew it would not be long before he became insistent.

Arriving at Darcy House, they gave their coats to the maids that waited and climbed the stairs. Elizabeth entered the dressing room first to prepare for bed while her spouse waited, his valet helping him remove his topcoat. He then took off his waistcoat and shoes, handing them to the servant to clean and put away. He put his watch on the bedside table before pulling his shirt tail out of his trousers. He then grabbed a book from the stand and sat in the chair by the fire, waiting for his opportunity to use the dressing room.

He read for what felt like a long time before suddenly realizing that his wife was taking longer to get ready for bed than she usually did. Already alert to the fact that she was behaving totally out of character, he was more convinced than ever that something had happened in the ladies' parlor.

He tried to recall the women he had seen leaving that room while he waited for her to emerge. As he listed them all in his mind, he remembered two very young ladies walking out of it not long before Elizabeth. They were not remarkable young women. They were obviously in their first season, probably only a few months older than his wife. Their looks did not catch his eye, but then, only his beloved seemed to have that ability. What struck him was their laughter. They had giggled and carried on as though they knew some great secret no one else was privy to. Whatever was going on in his spouse's mind had something to do with them, he was certain.

Finally, Elizabeth entered the bedchamber, apologizing for taking so long. She climbed into the bed, extinguishing the candle on her side as he left the room. A few minutes later, he joined her, reaching out to draw her to his side.

Kissing her softly in the dim light, he asked, "How did you enjoy your first ball, Sweetheart?"

"Very well," she answered quietly. "It was very tiring, though. I am exhausted." Her words were punctuated by a great yawn that felt like it was splitting her face.

"Yes, I am very tired, as well." He paused. "Elizabeth, I know that something happened in the ladies' retiring room. I can read the clues in your demeanor and behavior. I will not press you tonight, but tomorrow, we will discuss it. Do you agree?"

"Yes, Fitzwilliam. I love you."

"I love you, as well, my heart."

With a final kiss, the pair fell into a deep sleep, not to awaken until early afternoon the next day.

Chapter 4

Fitzwilliam slammed his fist into the wall of his father's study. He was as angry as he had ever been.

"Please, Son, calm yourself. I am as upset about this as you are. We will address it, but we must do so with clear heads."

"I am sorry for losing my temper in front of you, sir." He took a huge breath in before releasing it slowly. "I am amazed that daughters of society members are raised to think it acceptable to strike someone. Surely their parents do not know of this. They cannot condone it!"

"I doubt it. Think about when you went away to school. What kinds of things happened behind the teachers' backs? Did you never witness or experience abuse aimed at younger students by older ones? Girls go to school, as well. Do you think they do not perform the same types of acts against each other? If anything, I would think girls would be harsher on each other than boys; at least, if we take gentlewomen of high society as an example. They are a vicious bunch."

Fitzwilliam turned to stare at his father. "And you wish to send Georgiana to school?" he asked incredulously. "For what reason? To turn her into another violent female?"

Shaking his head, Mr. Darcy responded, "No; I would never want my dear daughter to become one of those kinds of women. However, she does need to learn how to navigate in society. I believe that I have taught her to be considerate of others, and I know that when you have been home, you have, as well. Not to mention the example she has in her sister. I have no fear of her abusing anyone." His voice turned wistful. "She has so much of her dear mother in her."

Fitzwilliam went silent, commiserating with his father without words. "Yes, she does. I miss Mother so much, still." He paused. "I apologize, Father. As always, you are correct. Please forgive me for questioning you. Georgiana could never behave as those young women did last night."

"I accept your apology. I appreciate that you are as protective of your sister as you are of your wife. One day, you will be the same with your own children. Hopefully that day will be soon."

Fitzwilliam rolled his eyes at his father's oft-repeated hint that he wanted grandchildren. Really, he could be such a woman at times, he thought. "Yes, well, when that happy day finally comes, you will be the first we share it with. Now, to get back to the business at hand; what are we to do about this insult to my wife? It must be stopped now. I will not let disrespect toward her go. If I do, it will continue and the violence will escalate. If it had been a man putting his hands on Elizabeth, I would have already called him out."

"Yes, and you would have been well within your rights to do so. However, these are young ladies, not gentlemen. You cannot call them out. What we can do, however, is speak to their fathers. We can make it clear that we will not tolerate such behavior in the future. Come, let us go to Matlock House and speak to your aunt. I am sure she will be able to tell us exactly who those young ladies were."

Within a short period of time, the pair were knocking on the door of the Fitzwilliams' house, having spoken to Elizabeth before leaving their own, assuring her of the shortness of their time away. She remained in her rooms for a long time with cold cloths on her face, only leaving it to spend a few minutes with Georgiana and only after rehearsing her response to the girl's anticipated questions about the handprint on her cheek. Georgiana was appalled that a lady would do such a thing. Elizabeth did her best to reassure her sister of her good health and that the bruise would surely fade in a day or so, and referred her to her brother or father for further information. At Georgiana's urging, Elizabeth returned to her room to rest and await Fitzwilliam's return.

~~~***~~~

Upon arriving at Matlock House, the Darcy men were shown into the drawing room, where the earl and countess were spending the afternoon togeth-
~~~

er in quiet pursuits. Surprised to see his brother and nephew, Lord Matlock rose to greet them.

"Darcy, Fitzwilliam, what brings you out after such an exhausting night? I thought you would be engaged as Audra and I are, in restful activities at home." He shook their hands and waited for them to greet his wife before continuing, "It is always good to see you, of course, but I can see by the look on my nephew's face that something has occurred. Tell me, then. What has happened?"

Fitzwilliam looked to his father to explain. They had decided between them to do so, the younger man not being sure of his ability to hold on to his temper due to his strong feelings on the subject.

Darcy cleared his throat before beginning. "We are here to ask about two of last night's guests. They were young ladies, one blonde and one brunette." Turning to his son, he asked, "Correct?"

"Yes, sir."

Nodding and looking back to the earl and countess, he continued, "These two ladies were the last to leave, prior to ourselves." Here he paused, ordering his thoughts. "Elizabeth was assaulted … slapped … by these two young women."

Lady Matlock gasped in horror. "What? When … how …?" She looked to her husband, who sat looking as shocked as she felt. "I am appalled! After all the measures taken to ensure her safety from that man, she is confronted by two girls! And in my house! Describe them to me!" She was quickly moving from shock to anger.

Fitzwilliam answered her, and his anger was clearly heard in his voice. "Both were young; they appeared not much older than Elizabeth. I have no doubt they are debutantes in their first season. The taller one was blonde, the other brunette. I saw them come into the foyer while I was waiting on her so we could leave. They were giggling and leaning into each other, carrying on in a very unseemly way."

"And you say they left just prior to the three of you?"

"Yes. I recall there were several people in the foyer awaiting their carriages. I do not know with whom these young ladies belong, however." Fitzwilliam spoke with great distaste for these unknown women who did not behave well.

Lord Matlock looked to his wife, "I believe we were speaking to Lord and Lady Blackmoore prior to George, Fitzwilliam, and Elizabeth leaving. Lord Blackmoore mentioned that they were waiting for their daughter and niece to join them, did they not?"

"Indeed, they did," exclaimed his wife. Turning to George, she said, "Lord Frederick Smith, the Viscount Blackmoore, and his viscountess, Lady Blackmoore. Their daughter, Cecilia, is out now. She performed her curtsey yesterday morning, along with Elizabeth, though she was presented early in the day. Their niece, Miss Diana Smith, was along, as well. She is the viscount's younger brother's child, and is staying with them this season, hoping to make a good match. Her father is rector in a parish in Sussex, I believe."

George nodded. "I know the viscount well. He is an honorable man, if a little too arrogant for my tastes. He is light-haired, as is his spouse; I assume, then, that Lady Cecilia is the one who struck Elizabeth."

"I wonder at the daughter of a rector being party to such goings-on," Fitzwilliam began. "What would her father say?"

"I do not know, Son. We were not there, though. Perhaps she was coerced by her cousin. I am certain there were times Richard and Trevor compelled you to do things, were there not?"

"Indeed," Fitzwilliam responded stiffly, "but never did it involve harming another person."

Lady Matlock responded, "Yes, but you must understand, girls are different than boys. Young men are more independent by nature, and society nurtures that. Girls, however, are more social creatures, and the approbation of others is important to us. Society limits what we, as females, can do and where we can go. Friendships and connections form the basis of our achievements, beyond our marriages. We are dependent on our friends and acquaintances for defining our place in society. It is not surprising that young girls often become followers more than leaders, and go along with schemes they might not otherwise, so as not to be ostracized."

"What of independent thought? One of the qualities I adore in my wife is her ability to think and analyze situations and come to logical conclusions. Surely all young ladies are encouraged to do what is right, what their consciences and the teachings of the Church indicate to them to do?"

"One would think so." Darcy shook his head. "Sadly, it seems that is not the case at times." Looking to his hosts, he said, "I thank you, Audra and Henry, for the information. I know where Lord and Lady Blackmoore reside; I believe my son and I have time to call there yet this afternoon." He rose, and the rest followed suit. "We will leave you now. Thank you again for your assistance."

"Happy to help," exclaimed Lord Matlock. "Let us know what the result of your visit is."

After taking their leave of their relatives, the Darcy men made their way to the Viscount Blackmoore's townhouse. Giving his card to the footman who opened the door, George Darcy asked to speak to the master of the house. He and Fitzwilliam waited in the foyer for just a few moments, before the footman reappeared and gestured for them to follow.

"This way, please, sirs."

A few steps down a hallway, he opened a door, stepped inside, and announced, "Mr. Darcy and Mr. Fitzwilliam Darcy." Once the men were inside he went back out, closing the door quietly behind him.

Lord Frederick Smith rose from behind a desk situated near a window in what appeared to be a library. Both Darcys took a quick glance around, but their focus was not on an appreciation for the room, but an explanation and satisfaction from the man who approached them.

"Darcy, Fitzwilliam, welcome to my home." Bowing to his guests, who bowed in return, the viscount gestured to a grouping of chairs near the fireplace. "Please, be seated, and tell me what brings you here today."

Darcy took a deep breath and began, "I am unsure how to go about this, so I ask that you allow me to say what I need to before you respond. Is that agreeable to you?" Upon receiving a nod from his host, he related his tale.

"When my family and I left the ball last night, my daughter was unusually subdued. At that time, she refused to tell my son what the matter was; however, this morning he insisted she do so."

He took another breath, looking at his clasped hands before raising his eyes to look at Lord Blackmoore again before explaining the events. Finally, he said, "As she was preparing to leave the withdrawing room, two young ladies entered and began speaking to her. At the end of this conversation, one of the ladies slapped my daughter. Twice. The two who assaulted her in this infamous manner were about her age, perhaps a little older. One was light-haired, the other dark. My son and I," he nodded to Fitzwilliam, "just came from Matlock House, where we inquired of Lady Matlock the identities of the young ladies."

Looking the viscount in the eyes, he clearly stated, "Your daughter, Cecilia, was one, and her cousin was the other."

Lord Blackmoore opened his mouth to speak,

but Darcy cut him off. "Fitzwilliam observed their return to the foyer just a few moments before Elizabeth's, and we were the last to leave, following shortly after your party. There is a bruise on her cheek, incontrovertible evidence that it occurred. It is I speaking to you and not my son, because his anger is so great. I am able to explain the events with a clearer mind, though you may be assured that I am just as angry."

"I am sorry, Darcy. As incredible as your story is, I do believe you. You are known to be an honorable, trustworthy gentleman, as is your son. You would not make such accusations without prior investigation." He rose, reaching for the pull to summon a servant. "Allow me to call my daughter down. I will get to the bottom of this, and you may be certain there will be amends made."

Mr. Darcy and his son both nodded. Their host

spoke quietly to the footman who answered his ring, then offered his guests a tumbler of port. Before they were finished with their refreshments, a knock was heard, and Lord Blackmoore bid the person to enter.

"You wanted to see me, Papa?" Miss Smith was curious, but not uneasy about being called to speak to her father. She was startled to see that he had guests, though.

"Yes, Cecilia, I have some questions for you. Come." He gestured her closer, and when she arrived at his side, introduced the gentlemen to her. The look on her face in that unguarded moment when she realized who the visitors were and likely why they were there gave away her guilt.

"I can see from your reaction to the gentlemen that their tale to me is true," he informed her sadly. "Why would you do such a thing? And do not give me a pretty tale. You will not get out of this with dissembling stories or blaming others. You left Mrs. Darcy with an injury. More than one, in fact. Where did you learn to behave so?"

His anger was rising with every moment that his daughter remained silent and expressionless. He continued to question her, his voice displaying more and more displeasure. It was not until he threatened to disallow further amusements and confine her to the house that she began to break. Her response was vehement.

"I did it because she does not belong in our circle! She is a fortune hunter! She has no dowry, no education. She is a laughingstock! Penelope said …"

Here her father cut her off, "Penelope? What has she to do with this? Do not dare to blame your behavior on your cousin. Regardless what she said or did not say, you acted on your own. You had a thought to attack Mrs. Darcy, and you did it. And then there is Diana! How did you convince her to go along with you? She is too sweet a girl, and too well-brought-up to do such a thing on her own. No, do not answer. I will call her down separately, after I am finished with you."

The viscount paced the room, while his visitors and his daughter watched. Fitzwilliam was struggling with a strong desire to turn Miss Smith over his knee and paddle her backside. It was apparent to him that the child, who in his opinion was behaving very badly, had never been corrected before. Only his training as a gentleman kept him in his seat and his hands to himself.

His father kept a keen eye on all the principals in the room, especially Fitzwilliam. While he trusted his son to behave properly, the young man was very angry, and angry people often did stupid things.

Finally getting control of himself, Lord Blackmoore addressed his daughter, who stood in the middle of the grouping of chairs, having not been invited to sit by her father. Her head was defiantly held high.

"Cecilia, I am ashamed of you. Your mother and I taught you better than this. Where is your compassion? Instead of disparaging Mrs. Darcy, you should be embracing her, making friends with her. Regardless of her roots, she is Mrs. Darcy. No, she is not as high as Lady Penelope, but her husband and his father are powerful men in our society, and you know this. They sit here now, just beyond you, and demand justice for their wife and daughter. Think of this … what if it were a royal who behaved in such a manner with you? How would you feel? You are far below such a person. Does that make you less than they? Would you not be upset and angry and expect me to demand recompense?"

A glance at his daughter showed that she did not believe such a thing could ever happen to her, and that she felt no remorse. Shaking his head, he continued, "You will, of course, apologize to Mrs. Darcy. And you will publicly welcome her into your circle. You will need to earn her trust, of course, and she may reject your apology. In any case, you will do as I say. In addition, you will remain at home for the next two weeks. No shopping, no balls, no dinners, no outings of any kind. Further, you will write an essay … five thousand words … on the benefits of kindness and the drawbacks of meanness. Your reading material will be restricted to certain sermons, of my choosing."

Miss Smith burst out, "No balls! But Papa …"

"Enough, Cecilia! Obviously you remain unmoved from your position, and unrepentant. Need I add more to your punishment so that you see your errors? Indeed, I feel I must. Therefore, you are restricted from the pianoforte and from receiving visitors for the duration of your period of punishment. You will spend this time in quiet reflection and study. I expect at the end of this fortnight that you will understand the effects of your actions on yourself and on your victim, and that your attitude will have changed. Do I make myself clear?"

Miss Smith swallowed. It was apparent to her that her father was deadly serious; she had never seen him so angry, not at her. "Yes, sir."

"Furthermore, when you have proven that you are repentant and understanding and are finally allowed back in society, there will be no repercussions to Mrs. Darcy for telling her husband what you did. It is his place to ask questions when he suspects something is wrong with her, and her place to answer his queries. She is not a schoolmate, and this is not an academy for young ladies. This is the adult world, and you will act like an adult, or those restrictions will be in force permanently."

By this time, the young lady was looking at her hands, which she had clasped before her. "Yes, Papa, I understand."

"Before I dismiss you, you will apologize to Mr. Fitzwilliam Darcy and to Mr. Darcy."

She turned to Fitzwilliam. "I am sorry for disparaging your wife, sir."

"That is all you are sorry for?" His deep, disapproving voice and stern countenance made her nervous.

"No, sir, I am also sorry for confronting her and for slapping her."

Fitzwilliam looked at her for a long moment. He felt in his heart that her words did not match her feelings; however, he chose to be gracious and accept her apology. He followed with, "My wife is the person who needs to hear these words. Be assured, Miss Smith, that any further insult will be met with greater consequences than those you are currently receiving. I cannot punish you as your father is, but I can ruin you in society, and I will not hesitate. My wife is my main con-cern. Her well-being is uppermost in my mind, and I do not care who I hurt to protect that."

Cecilia lowered her eyes to the floor. This man was beginning to truly frighten her. "Yes, sir," she responded, as respectfully as she could manage. Turning to Darcy, she apologized to him, as well. He responded, in her opinion, far more graciously than his son had. Thanking the two, she turned to her father once more.

"Papa?"

"I have rung for a footman. I will ask him to send Diana to me in the drawing room. You will wait here until she has come down, then you will go to your rooms. Your maid will be instructed to remove all reading material and music, and place it in my keeping. You will wait in your chambers, contemplating our discussion here, until you are called to dine. I expect unquestioned obedience. Am I clear?" At her nod, he dismissed her.

"Darcy, Fitzwilliam, I apologize for my daughter's actions. I will apologize to Mrs. Darcy, and bring Cecilia around to do so, as well."

Mr. Darcy nodded. "Thank you. I appreciate your

prompt and decided response. I am certain my son does, as well." He turned to Fitzwilliam.

"Yes, Father, I do. Lord Blackmoore, let me add my thanks. I must stress, though, that I was serious when I told your daughter that further attacks of any kind on my wife would be met by me with swift and decided consequences."

"And you would be well within your rights to do so. If she were a man, you could have called her out. I will impress that upon her even further. Thank you for your graciousness."

Soon, the gentlemen took leave of each other, and the Darcys departed for home.

~~~***~~~

Upon their arrival at Darcy house, Fitzwilliam asked the footman for his wife's whereabouts. Hearing that she was in their rooms, he quickly
~~~

ascended the stairs, as his father watched with a smile and a shake of his head. I remember being so eager to see my Anne, he thought. I am glad he shares a similar marriage with Elizabeth.

Arriving at the chambers he shared with his spouse, Fitzwilliam quietly turned the handle and entered the room, closing the door behind him with a soft click. Seeing that she was not in the sitting room, he strode across the apartment to the bedchamber, peeking in and smiling widely to see Elizabeth lying on the bed, covered with a quilt, soundly asleep. Creeping into the room, he removed his topcoat and waistcoat, draping them over a chair, before sitting and removing his boots. When he was done, he gently lay on the bed, lifting her blanket and curling up behind and around her. Holding her close, he nuzzled her hair, breathing in the lavender scent she favored, before bestowing a kiss and laying his head behind hers.

The pair slept for a short while, Fitzwilliam awakening when his wife began to stir. Kissing her cheek and squeezing her tightly, he watched in fascination as she began to awake. This was a view he never tired of. She appeared so peaceful in sleep, younger than her sixteen years. With her poise and grace, she always seemed so much older when awake. As she became more aware, her nose twitched and her mouth opened and closed as though she were tasting something. Her eyelids began to flutter, and soon she began slowly blinking. Finally, she opened her eyes fully, saw him watching, and smiled as she stretched.

"Good afternoon, my love." Fitzwilliam leaned in to kiss her.

"Good afternoon," she replied. "Have you been home long?"

"Long enough to enjoy a short nap with my beautiful bride." Another, longer, kiss accompanied his statement, along with a nuzzle of her nose with his. "Did you sleep well?"

"Yes, I did. I did not realize how exhausted I was. How was your business?" Elizabeth was a little wary of his response. She knew he was furious about last night's incident, and she was nervous about what he might have done or said in response. She knew Papa George would do his best to keep him calm, but an angry Fitzwilliam was a frightening one, and there was no telling what he could have said or done.

"It went well. We decided before we left that Papa would do the speaking, as I was, and remain, far too angry to do it myself. However, my disapprobation was clear, I believe. Miss Smith certainly appeared frightened enough when I finally did speak to her."

Elizabeth laughed. "Did you turn the Darcy glare on her, my darling? It is a wonder she did not turn into a pillar of salt!"

Fitzwilliam chuckled. "If only I had such power! Alas, she remains flesh and blood. However, her father has set severe strictures on her activities for the foreseeable future. Her opportunities to assault innocent ladies are non-existent, as she is restricted to Blackmoore House. She is allowed no visitors, no pianoforte, and no reading other than sermons her father selects for her. There is more, but the salient point is that she is being punished, and that you may expect her to call on you to apologize at some point, and to publicly accept you into her company, when she is allowed out again."

Elizabeth was silent.

"My love?" He peeked around to look at her expression. "What thoughts are tumbling around in that gorgeous head of yours?"

"Will she mean it? If she is forced to apologize, how do I know it will not happen again? She implied, if it can be called that, severe consequences if I told you what happened, and I did just that."

"Sweetheart, look at me." He rolled her to her back, still held in his embrace, and looked her in the eye. "It was made clear to her by her father that, as my wife, it was your duty to tell me, especially when I noted something was wrong and inquired of you what it was. He further stressed that to threaten you again was to risk more sanctions. I also made it clear to her that I would ruin her socially if such a thing occurred, and believe me, I will. The Darcy name is a powerful one. I don't know if you understand just yet how power-ful it is. I certainly do not. Every meeting I attend with my father drives the point home to me that people listen to him, to us. We do not go pushing our will on others, but when the situation calls for it, we make sure we are heard. She will be sincere in her apology, I promise you."

Elizabeth smiled tremulously. "What would I do without you, my Fitzwilliam? You take such good care of me. Thank you for being my defender and my protector. I love you."

Her husband leaned down and tenderly kissed her lips. "I love you, Sweetheart. I will defend you to the death. You are my life." He kissed her again, and the couple soon gave in to the passion that always seemed to flow when they were together.

Chapter 5

The Darcys remained at home for several days while the bruise on Elizabeth's face healed. The only visitors they saw were family: the Fitzwilliams, and the Gardiners and Jane.

During this time, Elizabeth, when she was not supervising Georgiana's education, entertaining family members, or spending time alone with her husband, took time to reflect quietly on the events of the ball. Her feelings on the night were murky. She knew without a shadow of a doubt that the biggest part of the evening was a success. She was introduced to many of her new family's peers, and managed to charm most of them. In the process, she discovered she had retained her ability to draw people out with a quip and a warm smile. She also realized that she was still able to use that same warm smile and witty remark to put someone in their place without them even realizing it. For the first time in what seemed like a long time, she felt a measure of confidence. Combined with the trust in her husband and Papa George and their ability to ensure her physical safety, at least from Lord Regis and his ilk, she was sure she could survive what remained of this social season.

Despite this, she retained some fear, and that feeling made her angry. Contemplating further, she realized what angered her was Lord Blackmoore's daughter and her actions. That a young lady she had barely been introduced to would accost her in such a violent manner was a shock in itself. That said young lady was the daughter of a viscount – a peer – was more so. Did she not go to school and learn proper comportment?

Before going to school, did she not have a governess to teach her how to behave when still a child? Where did she learn that striking someone was acceptable behavior? Elizabeth was the self-taught daughter of a minor gentleman, and even she knew to keep her hands to herself. Did Miss Cecilia Smith not pay attention in church? Surely she attended! The teachings of the church were clear that violence toward one's fellow man was not acceptable. So who did she think she was?

And why? Why did this young woman target her that way? What had Elizabeth ever done to Cecilia to give her cause to confront her? Elizabeth looked in the mirror. Fitzwilliam told her constantly that she was beautiful, but she knew from listening to her mother for sixteen years that not everyone believed she was. Cecilia was the classic English beauty: tall, thin, and blonde.

Elizabeth was short, dark-haired, and curvy. There was nothing striking about her; no reason for anyone to be jealous of her looks. It could not be that she did not like Elizabeth's personality or something she had said; the pair had not spoken to each other beyond a greeting. It could not be her clothing, for Elizabeth knew from Lady Matlock that they shared the same modiste. The only conclusion she could come to is that Cecilia was mean, plain and simple. And that added to Elizabeth's agony and anger. There was no reason for the attack. Elizabeth was simply there at an opportune time.

The more Elizabeth thought about it, the angrier she got. She paced the room, beat her fists on her thighs, and began eyeing the china figurines on the mantelpiece. Surely the sound of them breaking on the hearth would make her feel better! But no, that would create more work for the maids, and she did not want to do that. They should not suffer for her amusement. Finally realizing that physical activity would relieve her emotions, she sought out her husband.

Finding him in the library, she approached with a soft smile and perched herself in his lap, her arm around his shoulders.

Fitzwilliam chuckled as she settled in, laying his book on the table beside him before kissing her softly.

"Good afternoon, Sweetheart. To what do I owe the pleasure of your company?"

"Can a girl not cuddle with her beloved husband without cause?" Elizabeth asked with a twinkle in her eye and an arch to her brow.

"Hmmm. Perhaps." Another kiss, slower this time, and more thorough. ""Mmmmm. How did you know I was thinking of you?"

"You were thinking of me? I am flattered, Fitz-william. I thought you were contemplating …" She reached over and snatched his book off the table. "Pope?"

"No," he denied, drawing the word out. "Pope is just a cover for what I am really thinking about." He kissed her again. "Lavender." Kiss. "Soft lips." Kiss. "Warm hugs." Kiss.

She giggled. "Really, my darling?"

"Really." A final kiss and then he sat back, giving her the look she knew meant that she needed to be forthcoming about whatever was on her mind. She sighed and he smiled, recognizing the sign of surrender for what it was.

"I have been thinking about … things. I am angry, and need to release it somehow. If I were at

Longbourn, I would walk, perhaps to Oakham Mount. However, I am in London, and I have a handprint on my cheek. That would not be a problem, except there is no place to walk where there are no other people. It is a conundrum. I came to you hoping you would find a solution. Perhaps we could go race the horses again?" She looked hopefully at him.

Fitzwilliam hugged her tightly. He understood her desire to release her feelings through physical activity. He utilized that method frequently, going to his fencing and boxing clubs, as well as riding and occasionally walking. He also knew she chafed at being restricted in her movements. In the months she had been in London – weeks before their marriage with her aunt and uncle Gardiner, then weeks since their marriage here at Darcy House – she had rarely set foot outside except to shop or attend church. She had her presentation and her ball and had made some calls with his aunt, but that was it. She had had no opportunity in weeks for exercise, other than that one day they had raced the horses on the outskirts of the city.

Releasing her enough that he could see her face, he finally responded. With his hand rubbing up and down her back, he said, "You do need some activity, this I know. You have been housebound too long." He sighed, pausing to order his thoughts before continuing. "I believe I know a place we can go and walk, away from prying eyes. I will ask Cook to prepare a picnic basket, and we can spend the entire afternoon there. What do you think? Is this acceptable?"

Elizabeth smiled widely, delight overtaking her features. She threw her arms around his shoulders once again, exclaiming, "Oh, Fitzwilliam, it sounds delightful! Thank you, my darling! I knew you would find a solution!"

Her husband laughed, pleased he had made her happy. "Go on with you now. You must change your clothes, and I must arrange things with the coachman and cook. I will meet you in the foyer in an hour."

She hopped up from his lap, blew him a kiss, then rushed from the room to go to their chambers and change.

~~~***~~~

Hours later, the couple sat cuddled together under a tree in a field far outside London. The remains of their picnic lunch lay at their feet at the end of the blanket they sat on, and their shoes and stockings, as well as Fitzwilliam's topcoat and waistcoat, were piled in a corner.
~~~

"Thank you, my darling, for bringing me here. Who knew such an empty place existed so close to town? The walk in from the road was so invigorating! It was just what I needed to restore my good humor!"

"You are welcome, Sweetheart. Did you enjoy running through the meadow, as well?"

"Now, you know that I always enjoy being chased by the handsomest man in England," she responded with a laugh, leaning in for a kiss.

Her husband joined in her laughter. They continued to sit there, talking about the ball and Elizabeth's muddled feelings, kissing now and again. Their passions rose, and they enjoyed the pleasures of one another, finally falling into sleep, arms wrapped around each other. After a short period of rest, they noticed the sun falling far down in the sky. The pair redressed themselves, packed up their picnic things, and began the long walk back to the carriage, refreshed, renewed, and ready to handle anything that came their way.

~~~***~~~

Finally, the day came that the evidence of Miss Smith's assault was no longer visible on Elizabeth's face. She and Fitzwilliam, along with Papa George, had been invited to a dinner party at the home of one of Mr. Darcy's friends.

As they waited in the foyer, Fitzwilliam's father asked him how Elizabeth felt about their attendance at the event.

"She says she is not afraid, but judging by the look in her eye, she is at least apprehensive." He sighed before continuing, "We talked a long time the other day when we were on our picnic. She is pleased with the impression she made at the ball;
~~~

she feels it and she were a success. However, she is hurt and angry about Miss Smith's words and actions. She cannot understand the girl's motives. We discussed every possible reason, those we could think of, and have come to the conclusion that she is simply unkind. This makes Elizabeth angry, of course, for there was no reason for it to happen. But I believe her anger goes beyond Cecilia Smith. She has not said explicitly, but I believe she is still angry with Regis, and with herself for being fearful."

"She must watch that she does not become bitter. Unforgiveness is a terrible thing. She must forgive Regis and this young lady, but she must also forgive herself for being afraid."

"Yes, I have suggested as much to her. It is in her hands now. I can and will protect her from any form of future attack, as I know you will, Father, but I cannot protect her from herself."

Looking toward the staircase and seeing Elizabeth descending, he smiled and stepped towards her with his hand outstretched. She took his hand as she stopped on the last step. Raising hers to his lips, he kissed it, then leaned in and caressed her lips. "You are stunning, my love. Every guest in attendance will fall at your feet. The women will all want the name of your modiste and the men will all be envious of me."

Blushing and looking at her feet, Elizabeth rebuked him. "Fitzwilliam, stop. You know that is not true."

He tilted his head to look at her face, then used his free hand to lift her chin so he could see her expression clearly. "In my eyes, you are the most stunning creature I have ever beheld. And, since my opinion is the only one that matters, it follows that it must be true. It cannot be otherwise. Am I not correct, Father?"

Mr. Darcy smiled at the pair. "Yes, Son, you are correct. Daughter, you are indeed beautiful, and every person in the room will be envious. I am so proud of you for carrying on when you could be hiding in your room. No one would blame you if you did, you know. Yet, you face each new day with determination. If Georgiana shows half your pluck at your age, I shall be well-pleased.

"You are aware, are you not, that tonight's dinner is hosted by an old friend of mine?" Seeing Elizabeth's nod, he added, "I have known Jackson forever. He is predisposed to like you, and if you charm him as you have every other man in this family, he will sing your praises to everyone he sees. You are very like his late wife, Horatia. She was very witty, with just a hint of impertinence about her. So, please, do not be uneasy.

All will be well."

Elizabeth hugged him tightly, teary-eyed. "Thank you, Papa George," she whispered. "I love you."

"I love you, too, my dear." Letting go of her, he handed her back to her husband, joking, "There you go, my boy. Thank you for letting me borrow her for a minute."

Fitzwilliam rolled his eyes before replying, "You are welcome, Father. But perhaps you might ask next time, before you 'borrow' her?"

The trio laughed and Mr. Darcy slapped his son on the back, then they stepped out the door and into the carriage to travel to their event.

~~~***~~~

"Darcy, welcome to our home!" Mr. Adam Jackson exclaimed as he gripped his guest's hand, shaking it vigorously.
~~~

Grinning widely, Darcy returned the grip. Though he and Jackson had known each other since they were boys, it had been months since they had seen one another. It was good to be in each other's company again. Both looked forward to an enjoyable evening.

Letting go of the elder Darcy's hand, Mr. Jackson greeted Fitzwilliam just as enthusiastically. He was gentler with Elizabeth, but the warmth of his welcome could not be denied. She was able to relax a little, knowing her host was so accepting of her. When the gentleman introduced her to his hostess, his eldest daughter, Mrs. Evander Standford, Elizabeth was able to relax even further, for Mrs. Standford was every bit as warm and welcoming as her father.

"Please, call me Laura," she urged. "I just know we shall be great friends! Fitz and I grew up together, you know. Well, he was more the friend of my brothers, but as the eldest, I made sure I was invited along on their adventures." Winking at Elizabeth, she laughed gaily.

With a giggle of her own, Elizabeth glanced at her husband before leaning toward her new friend and demanding, "Oh, you must share some of those adventures with me! Fitzwilliam has told me much, but I would love to hear of them from a different perspective! And please, you must call me Elizabeth."

The two chatted a few moments longer, until other guests arrived and the Darcys moved into the drawing room. There, they mingled with the newcomers until their hosts joined them.

Elizabeth was feeling rather relaxed. She had met almost everyone in the room previously; all were people she felt looked upon her with kindness, if not friendliness. She was beginning to truly enjoy herself when she was suddenly confronted with one of the people she wished never to see again – Lady Penelope Mays.

"Mrs. Darcy," she sneered in greeting. "Imagine finding you here." She lowered her voice. "Did my cousin not teach you enough of a lesson? You needed to come back for more?"

Stiffly, Elizabeth replied, "Your cousin? I am sorry Lady Penelope, I have not the pleasure of understanding you."

Fitzwilliam, who stood beside her with his arm wrapped in hers, had felt her stiffen and quickly brought his conversation to an end. Turning his attention to his wife, his eyes narrowed when he saw the person speaking to her. When Penelope lowered her tone, he leaned his head down to better hear her conversation. The lady appeared not to even notice he was there, so intent was she on threatening Elizabeth. Such was her arrogance that she was convinced he would despise his wife and begin leaving her at home rather than face the derision of society. She was about to find out just how wrong she was.

Lady Penelope had continued in the low voice she had taken, almost whispering, "Do you not? Did Cecilia not demonstrate to you how low you are? I know she did, for she is my young cousin and always does as I ask. Shall I remind you of her actions and words? I daresay if she did not leave enough of an impression, I certainly can."

Before his dearest spouse could respond, Fitzwilliam spoke in clear, cold, carrying tones. "Lady Penelope, what is this you are telling my wife?" The lady froze. "You instigated an assault upon her?" He paused, waiting for her response, and when she remained still and did not open her lips, he demanded, "Answer me!"

Lady Penelope glanced around, swallowing when she realized a large portion of the room's occupants had heard him. Raising her chin in a gesture of defiance, she replied. "I do not know what you are speaking of. I? Instigate an assault on someone? Surely you are joking!" She laughed in an attempt to appear unafraid, but it sounded weak to even her own ears. However, she was not ready to give in yet. She was a Mays, after all, and the daughter of an earl. She was a member of the peerage. He was only a landowner. In her attempt to save face, she forgot that, though only a landowner, Mr. Fitzwilliam Darcy and his father were very powerful men.

"I warned your cousin what would happen should there be any more assaults, of any kind, upon my good wife. Lord Blackmoore must have followed through with the punishment he laid out for Lady Cecilia if you are unaware of the consequences."

Lady Penelope swallowed again but maintained a stoic expression. The coldness of Mr. Fitzwilliam Darcy's voice, combined with the hardness in his eyes, made him a very intimidating gentleman. She saw him shift and realized that his father had joined them, on the other side of Mrs. Darcy and with a demeanor similar to that of his son. The stances of both men made it clear to one such as she, who was well-versed in the nuances of high society, that their support was firmly with their wife and daughter. Lady Penelope was beginning to feel some apprehension. It was not supposed to have worked this way. Mr. Darcy spoke.

"Lady Penelope, what are you about?"

Suddenly she snapped. "What am I about? What are you about, sir? You have been taken in by a ragamuffin fortune hunter from a family of little consequence and miserable connections! You have connected your only son to a woman with relatives in trade. Have you no shame?" She paused to take a breath, but before anyone else could get a word in, she continued. "She does not belong among good society! She should be cast off, and I intend to make sure she is not received by the best families. If you will not see reason, I will ensure she does. You have an estate in Scotland, I believe … that is where she should go, a place far away where she can be hidden. She is shameful! Look at her! She has not a fine feature in her face, her figure leans to fat, and her voice grates. She is common, and I am doing all in my power to make certain she never loses awareness of it."

Red-faced and breathless, Lady Penelope finally stopped speaking. The room was deathly silent, every breath held to see what the response of the Darcys would be to such a terrible accusation toward one of their own. They were known to be fiercely protective, and many in the crowd were silently sure that if she were a man, the lady would have been called out by now. They did not have long to wait.

In a voice so cold that everyone in the room shuddered, Mr. Darcy began to defend Elizabeth. "Madam, my daughter is a gentlewoman. She is the niece of one of my closest friends, a tradesman whose wife is twice the lady you are. Your title holds no weight with me, nor does that of your father. I could buy your family twice over. Mrs. Darcy's dowry or lack thereof is no concern of yours.

"My daughter is the epitome of a lady in manner, dress, and comportment. She is one of the most beautiful women I have seen, second only to my late, beloved wife. She is proving herself to be a capable mistress of Darcy House, and I am convinced will excel even more when she begins her duties at Pemberley."

Fitzwilliam cut in, determined to have his say and to punish this woman who hated Elizabeth. In a voice and with a countenance every bit as cold, hard, and demeaning as his father's, he intoned, "You and your family, *Lady* Penelope, are no longer welcome in company with the Darcys. I personally will make certain the tale of your actions is known far and wide, and you will be the laughingstock. Not I, not Mrs. Darcy or our father, but *you*. If one of us sees you in the street, we will cross to the other side. Never again will you be acknowledged by any of us. If word of any further attacks reaches me or my father, rest assured, madam, that we will sue you for slander. Should they be physical assaults, I will have you arrested and sent to Newgate, you and everyone who assists you in any way. Is this clear?"

After receiving tongue-lashings from two such frightening men, all Lady Penelope wanted was to leave their presence and gather herself and her composure. It was not to be, however, for at her side appeared her host and her father, both with severe expressions.

"Penelope!" Lord Sheffield exclaimed. "What have you done?"

"Father, I ..."

"She insulted my wife, sir, and not for the first time. In addition, she instigated an assault by your nieces upon Mrs. Darcy's person at her presentation ball several days ago. Miss Smith injured and attempted to intimidate my wife into silence. It is not to be borne, and it will not be."

Darcy stepped in, seeing that his son was becoming increasingly angry. "Lord Sheffield, the Darcy family hereby cuts all ties with your own. An apology from your daughter is expected, but will not change our plans. Perhaps, sir, she could be sent to an estate in Scotland, as she suggested we do with Mrs. Darcy. As my son said earlier, if she were a man, he would have called her out and none would blame him, regardless of the outcome."

He stepped closer to Lady Penelope's father and lowered his voice. "Unless you want your daughter to remain unmarried and cast off from society, you will control her. Obviously, you have not to date. The promises my son and I have issued today are not idle, and you will soon reap the consequences."

Jackson spoke quietly to Lord Sheffield and Lady Penelope. "I think, sir, it is time for you and your family to leave."

The gentleman and his daughter looked at him in shock, speechless. Finally, to avoid any further confrontation and future gossip, he grasped Penelope's arm and pulled her from the room.

Jackson turned to Darcy. "George, I apologize. It is inexcusable that such a thing would happen to one of my dearest friends, and in my own house! I would not fault you if you desired to take Mrs. Darcy home, but I hope you will consent to stay and let me make amends."

Darcy, upon seeing the Mays family leave, let down his stance, relaxing the tense set to his shoulders and spine, as well as the severe expression on his face. He looked to his son, who turned to Elizabeth. She hesitated before giving an infinitesimal nod. She was greatly upset. Angry, even. However, she was a lady and was not about to stoop to the level of Lady Penelope. She would not contribute to the gossip if she could help it. Fitzwilliam, seeing her nod, gave one to his father, who turned to his host and replied, "Thank you, Adam; we would be delighted to stay." Looking at the other guests, who had yet to stop staring, he stated, loudly and clearly, "I have said this before and I say it again: Mrs. Darcy is my daughter, and any insult or injury to her is an insult or injury to me. I will not ignore either. Any man, or woman, who does not wish to be in our company, will be cut from our acquaintance just as Lord Sheffield and his family have been, and we will not repine. Your status means nothing to us. We do not need connections who would disparage us."

No one moved, other than to lower their eyes and nod. Most were friends of George Darcy and valued that relationship. The few that were not, were not about to put themselves into a position for him and his family to cut them.

The rest of the evening passed pleasantly, as all the guests made an effort to put behind them the scene they had witnessed in the drawing room.

Chapter 6

The next day, as the family broke their fast, they discussed the events of the previous night. This was something they always did, whether at Pemberley or in town. It gave the family, including Georgiana, an opportunity to express their emotions and concerns and to reassure and comfort each other. In the course of this day's conversation, it was suggested by Mr. Darcy that his newest daughter plan a dinner, an idea enthusiastically endorsed by Fitzwilliam. While reluctant, Elizabeth saw the sense in the plan, and knowing as she did Lady Matlock's willingness to assist her in any endeavor, she agreed to it. Immediately after the meal, a note was duly sent off to the lady, requesting her assistance and that of Lady Tansley.

An hour later, the two women arrived at Darcy House, prepared to assist Elizabeth in any way they could. The rest of the day was spent planning the menu and entertainments and compiling a guest list. The date was set for a se'ennight out, and a servant sent to the stationery shop for extra paper and ink. The ladies agreed to meet again early the next day to begin writing out the invitations, and Elizabeth would check this evening with her husband and father to finalize the list of names.

"I am proud of you, Elizabeth, for so willingly putting yourself forth in this manner," Vanessa said, squeezing her cousin's hand tightly. "Most of the ladies I know would hide away after receiving such treatment. I know Fitzwilliam must be so proud of you."

"Darcy is, as well, I daresay," Lady Matlock added. "He truly looks at you as a daughter, my dear. I think there is nothing you could do that he and Fitzwilliam would not overlook and excuse away." She smiled at her niece, who smiled back.

"Thank you, Aunt Audra. And you, Vanessa. My desire is to please my husband in all things, and by extension Papa George. Your words are a great encouragement to me." She rose from her seat, and her guests stood with her. She hugged each one tightly before reaching for their hands. "I love you both, very much."

Moved to tears by her quiet declaration and unused to such sentiments being spoken aloud in their society, all the ladies knew to do was squeeze her hands tighter before letting go and quietly leaving for home.

Once her guests had gone, Elizabeth took her list

and went to find her Fitzwilliam and Papa George, who, as expected, were working in the study. After knocking and being bid entrance, she paused in the doorway, watching them for a moment. Their heads were bent over a set of papers, pens in their hands, twirling between their fingers in identical motions. Combined with their similar coloring and features, it was as though she were looking at twins instead of father and son.

Her moment of admiration was fleeting, however, when one glanced up and saw her leaning against the doorframe. He quickly stood, and the other, seeing what was happening, followed suit.

Advancing toward his spouse, Fitzwilliam rounded the desk while reaching for her hands. "Sweetheart, what can we do for you?"

He led her to a settee beside the desk and sat her down, sitting as close beside her as he could get. He would have liked to set her on his lap in the chair he had been in when she entered the room, but with his father there, he thought better of the idea.

In danger of being lost in his eyes, Elizabeth forced hers away, though she held tightly to his hand and leaned on his shoulder, so he knew she felt as he did.

"I have a tentative guest list for the dinner party. Aunt Audra encouraged me to ask you and Papa George to look at it. You are free to make any additions or subtractions you wish; this is just to get us started."

Glancing at her father-in-law, Elizabeth's gaze was irresistibly drawn back to that of her husband. Her heart raced, as it always did when in close proximity to him.

Mr. Darcy cleared his throat, startling his children. He was quite aware that if he did not nip this staring thing in the bud, they would be insensible to anyone or anything else … and were likely to begin behaving inappropriately. While he was delighted with them both and with their felicity, he had no desire to witness it.

"If you hand your list over to me, my dear, I will peruse it first." He chuckled when her face became bright red, and she once again forced her gaze from his son's.

For his part, Fitzwilliam snaked his arm around his wife's waist, holding her tightly, as his face also crimsoned. This was not the first time his father had been forced to separate them, and while one would think he would be used to it, he was embarrassed to lack control in front of his father. It was just that he found Elizabeth so beautiful, and so sweet, and curvy, and she smelled so good … and her eyes and the love he could see there drew him in. He was powerless to resist her.

Darcy cleared his throat again before looking up from the page. "This is a very comprehensive list. Audra knows exactly who needs to attend any given event and who can be excluded. I do wish to add a couple names," he said as he picked his pen up once again and began scratching words out on the list. "There," he declared as he finished writing with a flourish. "Now, Son, it is your turn."

Taking the list from his father, Fitzwilliam examined it carefully. "I would like to add some names, as well." He counted the number of people and then asked if one more couple would be too many. When Elizabeth said two more people would be fine, he let her go, picking his own pen up and adding the names of one of his university friends and the man's wife. When he finished, he set his pen down upon the list, rose from his seat, and, holding his hand out to his spouse, excused them to his smirking father before leading her up to their chambers for a period of refreshment.

<div align="center">~~~***~~~</div>

The following week passed quickly. The ladies of Matlock assisted Elizabeth with every aspect of the dinner preparation, encouraging her along the way. Georgiana, desiring to be as helpful as possible, participated as much as her schedule of lessons allowed.

The staff was just as eager to assist their mistress, and worked very hard to scrub, dust, and polish every fixture and corner of the house to a shine. The cook was unused to preparing for such large numbers of people, but she rose to the challenge admirably, consulting her cooking books and planning recipe execution and delivery like an army general in charge of a battle. Mr. Baxter and Mrs. Bishop were as excited as schoolchildren to show off the house where they served in a way that had not been done since before Master Fitzwilliam's mother had passed away.

Finally, the night of the party arrived. As the family, minus Georgiana, who ate in the nursery that night, stood in the foyer ready to greet their guests, Elizabeth nervously smoothed out her skirt. Noticing the sign of anxiety, Darcy and Fitzwilliam both gave her words of encouragement. When words did not seem to help, Fitzwilliam decided she needed to relax a bit. Excusing them, he drew her into a nearby room, shutting and locking the door behind them before kissing her senseless. When he finally felt her lean bonelessly into him, he slowed the caress of his lips before drawing away. The sight of her half-lidded eyes and slightly swollen lips made him smile, and he asked, "How are you feeling?"

"Wonderful," Elizabeth breathed.

Chuckling, he replied, "Then let us get you out there before the effect wears off." And so, he led her back out to the receiving line in time to greet the Matlock party.

Lady Matlock examined the pair with narrowed eyes. "What have the two of you been doing?"

"I took my wife into the other room for a few minutes. She was anxious and needed to relax. Her hair is not mussed, and neither is her gown. She is happy and at ease."

"Hmph," his aunt replied. "Anyone with eyes will guess how you relaxed her. You really should be more careful about these things, but since your father was aware of what was happening, I suppose nothing I can say will make a difference."

Her nephew only smiled and bowed, his hand settled against the small of the blushing Elizabeth's back, where his thumb rubbed up and down.

As Lord and Lady Matlock joined the receiving line, the first of the guests began to enter the house. Smiling graciously and glad that her husband had distracted her from her concerns, Elizabeth was able to greet each visitor with confidence. She curtseyed and smiled, asked after family members, and received comments and the inevitable subtle criticisms with grace.

The dinner itself went well. The staff did the family, especially the young mistress, proud. Every course was timed perfectly and served at the correct temperature. Sharp-eyed footmen made sure wine glasses remained full at all times, and the hosts kept the conversation flowing. It was only after the ladies retired to the drawing room that cracks began to show in the harmony of the gathering.

Not long after Elizabeth led the ladies into the room, a young woman approached her with a pinched look and her nose in the air.

"Mrs. Darcy."

The two curtseyed to each other.

"Miss Pennywhistle, how good of you and your family to attend our little soiree." Elizabeth smiled at her guest, though every warning gong in her head was sounding. She was sure this young lady was going to try to discompose her.

"I spoke recently with my close friend, Lady Penelope Mays … perhaps you remember her?" At

Elizabeth's nod, she continued, "I must say I agree with her estimation of you. You do not belong. I believe I will join her in her quest to remove you from our society."

More than a little surprised at the lady's bluntness, Elizabeth had nonetheless had enough. This was her home, and she would be dead in her grave before she was insulted here. She could feel her courage rise along with her anger.

Speaking in a low but vehement voice, she stated, "Indeed, madam. Are you aware of the consequences Lady Penelope and her family have experienced as a result of her foolish actions? The house of Sheffield is no longer recognized by the Darcys. How would your parents feel if your actions caused them to join that family in their exile from my family's circle, hmm? You realize, of course, that society as a whole will follow the Darcys. We may not be titled, but we are powerful. Beware, Miss Pennywhistle, beware.”

With a fiery glare at her guest, Elizabeth turned her back and walked away. Ladies Matlock and Tansley, who had joined the pair upon seeing the look on Elizabeth's face as she spoke, remained in place.

“Madam, be assured that my mother and I,” Lady Tansley gestured to Lady Matlock, “will report this incident to Mr. Darcy.”

Nodding in agreement, Lady Matlock added, “The house of Matlock stands behind the Darcys in their decision to cut the Mays family from their acquaintance. Lord and Lady Sheffield are aware of this. I am surprised your parents are not. However, they will be before this night is over. My suggestion to you is to begin thinking of ways to grovel before Mrs. Darcy, and perhaps win back her approval." She looked at her nails as she continued. "Not that I think it will help. Mr. Darcy and Mr. Fitzwilliam Darcy are very protective of her." Now she looked straight at the startled young woman before her.

"I do not know what they are teaching these days in girls' schools, but surely abusing your peers was not a subject your teachers taught you. Perhaps you should be paying more attention in church. You are a disgrace to society and to your family." With those words, Lady Matlock and her daughter mimicked their relative by turning around and walking away, joining Elizabeth on the other side of the room.

For her part, Elizabeth was outraged at the effrontery of Miss Mary Pennywhistle. She maintained her countenance and her speech in such a way that none of her guests knew her feelings, but angry she was. Her Aunt Audra and Vanessa took the first opportunity to inquire of her.

"Are you well, my dear?" Lady Matlock asked. "We heard that young woman, what she said to you. After you walked away, Vanessa and I added our two pence to the conversation."

Lady Tansley, nodding in agreement, added, "I am sure she will at least think twice before speaking to you again. I believe she was struck dumb to be taken to task by a countess and a viscountess all at once." The three laughed at this.

"Thank you so very much for your support! I am angry that she would make this attempt in my own home. What was she thinking? Or was she at all? Honestly, I do not understand people like that." Taking a deep breath, she continued. "I apologize. I should not express my anger in such a way and in such a place. Forgive me."

"No, no, all is well," Lady Matlock soothed, laying her hand on her niece's arm. "I admire your grace in this matter. I would, I am afraid, be allowing everyone within hearing distance know of my displeasure, were I you."

Elizabeth and Vanessa smiled at the image of the always poised and proper countess loudly declaring her unhappiness.

"Thank you, both of you. I could not do this without you. Let us be seated. I just saw a servant gesture to me; the men should be returning momentarily."

Before much more time had passed, the gentlemen did indeed join the ladies. Always vigilant where his wife was concerned, Fitzwilliam immediately noticed that she was unhappy. Heading directly to her side, he sat beside her, holding her hand and leaning over to whisper urgently, "What happened?"

"I found that I had to censure one of the young ladies, darling. I believe that I handled myself very well." Her chin came up, indicating to him her pride in her actions. "Our aunt and cousin supported me. I hope all will be well from here."

Fitzwilliam, from the moment she spoke the word "censure," had begun scanning the faces of the ladies, eyes narrowed, to see if he could determine the identity of the offender. It was apparent from the way she would not meet his eyes which lady's father would be visited on the morrow.

"Miss Pennywhistle?"

Elizabeth gasped. "How did you know?"

"She will not look at me." He turned to his wife. "You spoke to her?" At her nod, he asked, "What did you say?"

"That this is my home, and I would not accept abuse here, from anyone. I then informed Miss Pennywhistle of the consequences Lady Penelope and her family faced for speaking to me similarly."

"I am proud of you, and if we were not here, in the midst of our guests, I would demonstrate for you just how proud I am." He squeezed her hand even tighter, which, combined with the smouldering look in his eye, caused her heart to leap in her chest.

Leaning toward him, she whispered, "Perhaps later, after they have all gone home, you can do just that?"

"You may be assured of it, madam."

True to his word, the moment the last visitor left the house that night, Fitzwilliam whisked his wife up the stairs to their chambers. Dismissing his valet and her maid, they locked the doors to the bedroom before undressing each other and falling into bed. Hours later, they finally slept, sated and happy.

The next morning, Fitzwilliam and his father visited a very unhappy Mr. Pennywhistle, making clear the expectations for receiving future invitations from the Darcys. The next time the mortified Miss Mary Pennywhistle saw Mrs. Elizabeth Darcy, a heartfelt apology was extended by the one and forgiveness by the other, with the caveat that the incident was not forgotten.

Word soon spread through the ton that the new Mrs. Darcy was not to be trifled with. The remainder of the season, while not completely painless for Elizabeth, passed rather easily.

~~~***~~~
~~~

In another townhouse in Mayfair, while the Darcy men were calling on the Pennywhistles, the Watson household was quiet, except for the master's study. Harold Watson, otherwise known as Lord Regis, listened unhappily as one of his cronies from the House of Lords regaled him with recent gossip, central of which was news of the new Mrs. Darcy.

How he hated her, and everyone associated with her! At the same time, he hated himself for still wanting to possess her. Even now, he did not love her. He simply wanted to own her, and never before had he been prevented from obtaining what he wanted. A voice inside told him to go take her, to make her pay for his humiliation, but a stronger voice recalled to him the threats made by George Darcy. No, he said to himself, she is not worth the scandal. My position in society and seat in Parliament is too valuable to me, and Darcy is too powerful an ene-my to cross.

He was grudgingly grateful to the man, however. Not a word of gossip had escaped about him, the incident at the bookshop, or any other action he had taken in connection with her, a fact that went a long way toward proving just how much influence Darcy wielded.

He sighed to himself before turning his attention back to his guest. He must maintain appearances, not letting anyone know his feelings and mood. It was a game he had played every day of his life, for as long as he could remember. It would not be difficult to continue.

Chapter 7

Almost before the family knew it, spring had turned to summer, and the air in London became increasingly unpleasant. The Darcy family, like so many other wealthy ones, packed up house and traveled to their country home. However, before they went to Pemberley, they planned a stop to visit Elizabeth's family at Longbourn. She had not seen most of them in months, since her father sent her to London after Lord Regis' attack, before her marriage. Fitzwilliam and his father both believed it was important for her to visit them. She needed to at least try to make peace with her mother.

Elizabeth was not so sure about the whole thing. She would rather have gone straight to Derbyshire and dispensed with seeing her parents at all. She was grateful for her father's actions in saving her from further injury, but he let her mother wail and moan and scheme for two more weeks before he removed Elizabeth from the situation. Granted, she had been very ill those two weeks, but a broken cheekbone and some bruising would not have prevented her from traveling in a private coach. She felt in her heart that he should have taken action immediately to shield her from her mother.

Her mother. Now there was a woman she would happily avoid the remainder of her life. Mrs. Bennet had never been a loving parent; she had never held Elizabeth close or praised her or comforted her when she was sick or injured. No, her mother was only ever critical. The two were so far apart in intelligence and general outlook that their similar personalities were never noted.

Both were lively women. However, Mrs. Bennet's mean understanding left her bewildered by her second daughter's conversation and attitude. She blamed Mr. Bennet for the girl's intractability. If he had not insisted on educating her, the child would have been perfectly content to marry Lord Regis, and her brother Gardiner would not have been able to barter a marriage in London, thus depriving herself of the honor she was due as matriarch of one of the most prominent families in Meryton. It never occurred to her that Elizabeth had married into one of the most powerful families in all England. All she knew was the girl turned down a peer who had promised to care for the remainder of the family should Mr. Bennet die, only to turn around and marry a gentleman with no title at all! She simply could not understand it! Had her husband not sent the child away, Mrs. Bennet was sure the marriage could have been quickly made. She was frustrated and angry and had been for months.

The Darcys made good time on this first leg of their trip, arriving in Meryton in time to have afternoon tea with the Bennets. When the carriages pulled up, Mr. Bennet and the girls flocked outside to greet them. Fitzwilliam exited first, handing Elizabeth out. His father followed and helped Georgiana and her nanny disembark. Elizabeth was greeted with hugs and exclamations by her sisters. Mr. Darcy and Fitzwilliam hung back, waiting for the hullabaloo to die down so she could make introductions. Soon, she turned to them, tucking her hand in the crook of Fitzwilliam's elbow. She greeted her eldest sister first.

Jane, who had returned just three days ago, hugged Elizabeth tightly, whispering, "I have so much to tell you!"

Elizabeth smiled, then turned to the rest of her family. "Papa, Mary, Kitty, Lydia, this is my husband, Mr. Fitzwilliam Darcy, his father, Mr. George Darcy, and his sister, Miss Georgiana Darcy and her governess, Mrs. Northrop."

As her sisters curtseyed and her father bowed, she continued the introductions.

"Papa George, Fitzwilliam, Georgiana, Mrs. Northrop, this is my father, Mr. Thomas Bennet, and my sisters, Miss Jane Bennet, Miss Mary Bennet, Miss Catherine Bennet, and Miss Lydia Bennet." It was the Darcy party's turn to bow and curtsey.

"It is good of you to come, Mr. Darcy. I have missed my Lizzy, as have her sisters. I am eager to hear everything that has happened since I sent her to London. Please, come inside."

Darcy and his son looked at each other. Both had noticed that Mrs. Bennet had not come outside with the rest of the family to greet her daughter. Both were offended, but soundlessly communicated that silence was perhaps best at present. They followed as the group entered the home, Elizabeth having taken Georgiana by the hand. Her sisters, when taken as a group, could be a raucous bunch, and she designed to be close by at all times to remove the young girl, should the need arise.

Too, Elizabeth felt a need for the support of her new family. It had not escaped her that her mother did not greet her as the rest did. She had dreaded this day for months, and everything was going the way she had thought it might. The confidence she had begun to regain in the last few weeks was faltering. She could feel Fitzwilliam's eyes boring into her back, and was comforted by the support she knew she had from him and from his father.

Far too soon, the group reached Mrs. Bennet, who was sitting in Longbourn's drawing room. She rose from her seat as they entered, curtseyed when introduced, then sat back down, calling her dear Lydia to sit beside her.

The rest of the Bennet family, from patriarch to youngest child, were shocked and embarrassed that she could be so rude to anyone, much less the family that would likely be called upon to save her from the dreaded hedgerows.

Jane, red-faced and with her head hung low, gestured to their guests. "Please, everyone, be seated. Mama," she said, turning to her parent, "shall I call for tea?"

"If you must," Mrs. Bennet sniffed. "Though, why Lizzy should be treated as a guest, I have no idea. Ungrateful child."

Fitzwilliam, who had seated himself next to Elizabeth on a sofa, tensed. Only his wife's hand on his arm prevented him from speaking his displeasure.

On her other side sat his father, who was equally angered. He sat stiff as a poker, a look of disapproval on his face. Out of the corner of his eye, he had seen Elizabeth stop his son, and recognized that, despite his desire to protect, he must let his daughter handle her mother as she saw fit … for now.

What followed was a stilted conversation of about a half hour. Finally, to everyone's relief, Longbourn's housekeeper, Mrs. Hill, entered to announce that the visitors' rooms were ready, and the Darcys retired upstairs to refresh themselves. Mr. Bennet took advantage of this time to have a word with his wife.

"Mrs. Bennet, I would speak to you in my book room. Now, if you please."

With a huff, Mrs. Bennet followed him to his room, closing the door behind her when he bid her to.

"What could you possibly need now, Mr. Bennet?"

Angry at her words and seeing clearly for the first time the lack of respect she held for him and his position as her husband, he took a moment to gather his thoughts. Finally, he sat in his chair on the other side of the desk, leaned forward, clasped his hands on the desktop, and began.

"What are you about, madam? Do you think I am in ignorance of your slight to your own daughter, your flesh and blood? Not to mention that her husband and his father are of the first circles. The first circles, Mrs. Bennet. They could buy and sell Longbourn several times over, I am sure." He paused, waiting for a response. When he did not get one, he let out an exasperated cry. "Mrs. Bennet!"

Startled, his wife jumped a bit, but she knew better than to keep him waiting for a response.

"What do you mean, what am I about? I am about nothing. I see no reason to fawn over that girl. What did she do but marry against her family's wishes? She deserves no recognition at all, if you ask me."

"I have not the pleasure of understanding you. What do you mean she married against her family's wishes? I have not a problem with her marriage to Mr. Fitzwilliam Darcy. What member of her family does?"

"Mr. Bennet, you know she was supposed to marry Lord Regis. We agreed ..."

"No, we did not agree to anything." He leaned over his desk, jamming his finger into the top to make his point. "You agreed to it with that abusive rake. You did! Not I; and I am the one with the power to make marriages for my children, not you. Your position is to run the household, to arrange meals and supervise the staff. That is all you are to be doing. Do you understand me?"

Mrs. Bennet looked like she had swallowed something sour. Her face was scrunched and her eyes narrowed. She was unused to her husband giving her any directions whatsoever, and she did not like it now. However, he was her husband.

"Yes, I understand you."

"Good. I expect you to be a proper hostess to our guests. That includes treating your daughter with civility. Again I ask, do you understand me?"

Resentfully, she responded. "Yes, Mr. Bennet. I do."

"Good. Then you may leave. I appreciate your cooperation in this, and I am certain your daughter does, as well."

Mrs. Bennet left the book room fuming silently. For several days of the visit, she managed to hold her tongue and behave in a manner that garnered her husband's approval. However, part of her lack of understanding was rooted in an inability to remember anything for more than a few days.

The Darcys had been at Longbourn for four days. Elizabeth had shown her new husband off to many of the neighbors and shown him her favorite places. She also spent time with her sisters, filling a need she had not known she had and hearing all their news, especially Jane's that Mr. Bingley had called on her at the Gardiners'. Mrs. Bennet had been no different than she had in the past those few days, but today she seemed angry, snapping at Elizabeth, and quietly complaining about her guests. For hours, the lively conversation of Lydia and Kitty, and the quieter questions posed by Mary and Jane, kept their mother's behavior somewhat in check. As the day went on, however, her complaints became louder.

Elizabeth quietly persevered through it all, hoping her mother would remember and heed the warning she had received from her husband just days before. Her father had found opportunity to apologize to Darcy, Fitzwilliam, and Elizabeth after dinner the day they arrived and had assured them of Mrs. Bennet's good behavior. However, this day he was off with the Darcy men, riding about the estate and talking farming. His wife took his absence as license to give vent to her feelings.

Finally, though, Elizabeth had enough.

"Please, Mama, speak clearly. Are we in your way? Would you like us to leave?"

"I do not know what you mean." Mrs. Bennet sniffed. "I did not say you were in my way. Just like you to take a simple statement and turn it into something it is not. Ungrateful child."

"Excuse me? I have done nothing of the kind. You are the one complaining. And, what do you mean by saying I am ungrateful? How have I been in any way ungrateful to you?"

"How? Why, you rejected a perfectly good offer of marriage from a peer, that is how! Who did you think you were, refusing an offer of marriage from a man who promised to save us from poverty when your father dies? I will tell you who you thought – and still do, no doubt, think – you were. You thought you were better than Lord Regis.

Better than a peer! It is because your father let you read all that nonsense. Turned you all high and mighty. I had it all arranged! Stupid girl!"

Jane tried to intervene. "Mama …" Her efforts were too little, too late. She shrank back, the three youngest making themselves as small as possible in their seats, as well.

Mrs. Northrop quickly removed Georgiana from the room, taking her to the garden to walk. This was a personal matter, and should be dealt with privately, she felt.

"He frightened me, Mother, from the first moment I met him! He was rude and arrogant. And he struck me! What kind of a man strikes anyone, much less a woman? And what is worse is that instead of allowing me to heal, you sat at my bedside when I was ill and in pain and browbeat me over it. Do you think I am unaware that you gave that horrible man permission to try to compromise me?"

Mrs. Bennet startled. It never occurred to her that her daughter would discover that information, and if her daughter knew, then her husband assuredly did also. She wondered why he had not attempted to speak to her about it.

"I did it for your own good, and for mine! No one else would want you! Even your high and mighty Mr. Fitzwilliam Darcy did not really want you. He had to be forced into the marriage, and I am quite certain he will throw you over sooner rather than later for someone more pliable and ladylike. You are unattractive and crude and do not deserve anything better than to be beaten. It is too bad your father stopped him. He would have turned you into a proper wife, Lord Regis would have. But then, had you been the heir you were meant to be, none of this would have mattered. An educated son is expected. Not once have you ever behaved as a daughter ought, and then your father, taking to you as he did none of our other children, not even Jane. My most beautiful child received far less of his attention than she deserved, because he was enamored of you. You!"

"Mama, I am not …" Jane tried once more to deflect her mother's arguments, to no effect.

"And why, you may ask, was that? It was because you look so much like the cousin you were named after. I know she had her cap set at him, but I won him! His attention was all mine, until you came along and stole it back." Her tone became even more vicious the longer she spoke. "If you had been born a boy, I would not have minded the loss."

Elizabeth never had the chance to respond. The

men in her life had come into the house just in time to hear the last of Mrs. Bennet's tirade. When Fitzwilliam charged toward the drawing room, no one tried to stop him. He threw the door open so hard it banged against the wall and bounced back, leaving a hole in the plaster where the knob hit it.

Breathing fire and with a look in his eye that no one could possibly mistake for anything other than anger, he placed himself between his wife and mother-in-law and roared, "Enough! You have said more than enough, madam."

Turning to his Elizabeth, he quietly but tersely told her to order their belongings packed and their carriage brought around. That complete, he faced his mother-in-law once again, trusting that his wife would do as he requested. "Mrs. Bennet, you have finally given voice to your true feelings about your daughter, and I, for one, am glad of it, for it gives me leave to act as I see fit. Elizabeth is no longer a Bennet. She is a Darcy, and she is my wife. She is beautiful, witty, and charming. She is gentle and kind and has proven herself already to be a worthy spouse."

As he spoke, Fitzwilliam had been stepping closer and closer, and Mrs. Bennet had been stepping further and further back. Finally, she bumped into the back of a chair and could move no further. Her son-in-law did not stop his forward motion, however, until he was inches from her person.

"If you were a man, I would call you out. You are the crude one, Mrs. Bennet. You deserve no attention from someone as pure and sweet as Elizabeth." He paused a moment as he attempted to control his rage.

"If I have my way, you will have seen the last of your daughter. You will never be allowed in our homes. We will not attend events where you are present. Your grandchildren will be strangers to you. I will leave it to Elizabeth, but I will strenuously plead my case for it."

Backed into a corner, as it were, Mrs. Bennet lashed out. "You have no authority over your house, sir. Nor do you have authority over me! I will not be told who I will and will not see by anyone, much less a gentleman such as you," she sneered, her tone of voice and manner indicating her dislike of him. "Lizzy has failed in her duty to obey her parents. She has always been an undutiful child, and I will not be silenced about it."

Here she was interrupted by her own husband, who, seeing the increasing rage on the faces of the Darcy men, stepped in to save his wife from herself. "You may not feel the need to obey Fitzwilliam, but you will obey me, Wife. If your son has decided to withhold your daughter from your presence, I support him wholeheartedly. Am I clear, Mrs. Bennet?"

Before she could respond, Darcy stepped into the fray. "My son may not be master, but he and I are united in our desire to see Elizabeth treated with the respect she deserves. Fitzwilliam has made the decision to remove you from her life; if Elizabeth agrees, I stand behind them. You, Mrs. Bennet, will not be welcome in our homes, in that case. In the meantime, we will remove ourselves from yours as soon as the carriage is readied."

To Bennet, he said, "Sir, perhaps my son and I could join you in your study while we wait for Elizabeth. I believe we may have more to discuss."

"Yes, I believe we do, to my eternal shame." Ordering his wife to her rooms, then listening to her continuous protests as she ascended the stairs, he waited until the house was quiet once again before gesturing to the doorway. "Come, gentlemen, let us have a glass of port while we wait."

A half hour later, a knock was heard on the door, before it slowly opened to Elizabeth, dressed in traveling clothes. She looked to Fitzwilliam first, who gestured her in as he stood. As she drew near, he reached for her hand to pull her in close for a hug. "Are you well?" he asked in a whisper.

Just as quietly, she responded. "Yes. I am sorry it took me so long to prepare. I was shaking so hard I had to sit for a while. Jenny had to bring me a glass of wine to settle me. I needed you to hold me. Thank you for loving me, Fitzwilliam."

As she said these words, she let go a little to look at him. With a tender kiss, he tightened his hold, "There is no need to thank me. You are easy to love, Sweetheart. I am so sorry you had to hear words such as those. I wish we had been back a few minutes earlier; perhaps it could have been avoided." He paused, laying his cheek on the top of her head, then stated what he knew would cause pain. "I want to cut off contact between us and your mother. I will not stand for anyone hurting you. What say you?"

Elizabeth heard the regret in his voice and moved to reassure him. "Darling, you defended me, and protected me from more of her wrath. That is more than enough. I think we needed to have this confrontation, my mother and I." She paused, and pain was clear in her voice when she continued. "I will not fight your pronouncements, my love. I am weary of her constant barbs. I have never been good enough for her. She has never understood my love of books and learning and the outdoors. I was not quiet and demure, like Jane, or stunningly beautiful, like Jane and Lydia. Nor did I have high spirits like Lydia. I do not fit her mold, her idea of what a daughter should be. When she could not force me into it, I believe she grew increasingly angry. I love her, but it is clear to me that she does not return the sentiment. It is best, I think, for us to separate."

Fitzwilliam wiped her tears, while in the background their fathers wiped their own. Bennet was struck with the truth of her statements. He had been blind to the effects of his wife's antics on his favorite daughter, not realizing until now the hatred behind them. He was grateful that Fitzwilliam had allowed him and the daughters who were still at home to remain part of Elizabeth's life. To have lost total contact with her would have been miserable.

Finally, Darcy spoke. "Children, the coach has

been brought around and the luggage loaded. We should begin our journey."

To Bennet, he said, "I thank you, sir, for your hospitality. Gardiner warned me repeatedly of what might happen, but we had to come. Elizabeth needed to see her family and share the place where she grew up with us. I hold no animosity toward you for your wife's behavior." He looked to his son. "I am sure Fitzwilliam does not, either."

"No, I do not. I have seen over the last few days the attempts you have made to control Mrs. Bennet. I had begun to hope the entire visit would go well. I thank you for making the effort, and I look forward to seeing you again, whenever you can make the trip." He shook his father-in-law's hand, then stood back to allow his wife to farewell him.

"Papa," she whispered, kissing his cheek and wrapping her arms around his middle as she had done as a little girl. "I love you. You will visit us?"

Holding her close, he laid his cheek on her head and quietly replied. "I love you, as well, my Lizzy. I am so sorry I never saw before what was really happening. I will visit when I can, I promise. You have married a good man. You will be well taken care of. And, I am proud of the woman I see here before me. You are beautiful, daughter. Do not let your mother's words convince you otherwise. You are more than capable. Your new family has shared many stories with me of your experiences. I look forward to hearing more in the future." He smiled, teary-eyed, before letting her go back to the grasp of her spouse. Speaking to the group, he wished them a safe trip before escorting them outside.

Before entering the coach, Elizabeth hugged each of her sisters tightly, whispering in their ears how much she would miss them, and giving advice on how to behave. Her sisters cried, clinging to her tightly, before reluctantly letting go and wishing her well.

Once she entered the coach, Elizabeth was hugged again, this time by Georgiana. She and Mrs. Northrop had returned to the house once the sounds from within had quieted, sitting in the drawing room where the confrontation had occurred. Upon hearing Elizabeth come down the stairs, they had retired to the waiting coach, knowing Darcy would have them on the road quickly.

With a quiet thank you and an explanation that she would rather not discuss it now, she settled her worried sister-in-law in beside her father on the opposite side of the vehicle. Back in her seat, she cuddled up to Fitzwilliam, breathing a sigh of relief when his arm came around her shoulders to hold her close.

Soon, the Darcys were back on the road to Pemberley.

~~~***~~~

While Elizabeth and her husband and father-in-law were talking to Mr. Bennet, his other daughters gathered in Mrs. Bennet's rooms, at her insistence. She required their presence to soothe her, not anticipating that their feelings would be so different from hers.

"My poor nerves," she wailed as she fanned herself with her handkerchief. "To be treated so poorly in my own home! It is not to be borne!"

Lydia looked at Kitty and rolled her eyes. This was not a new activity for them. Whenever their
~~~

mother did not get her way, she took to her bed to cry and moan, insisting on gathering her brood to attend her. Generally, they were able to ignore her, though it was not unusual for Lydia to stir her up for a laugh. Elizabeth was not the only one to inherit her father's traits. Today, however, none of the girls were amused. They were enjoying Lizzy's visit, having not seen her in months, and none were happy with Mrs. Bennet's tirade, nor did they understand her anger. Lydia, being Lydia, was the first to interrupt her mother's diatribe.

"Oh, stop, Mama! I do not understand what you are going on about! Lizzy married a very handsome and very rich man. Is that not what you have been after us to do for as long as I can remember? Is that not our entire goal in life? You pushed Jane and Lizzy both out at fifteen. All I have heard since is that I will soon be out and that I am so beautiful that I am sure to find a rich husband and save us all from the hedgerows. Come to think of it, you have said the same to Jane. What is so wrong about Lizzy being the first?

"I was enjoying her visit, you know. But you had to …" She waved her hand around, searching for words. "… blurt out everything in your head and ruin it for all of us. I do not understand why you are angry with her. You hate her, I know you do … you as much as admitted it! Do you hate me, as well? What about Jane, or Mary, or Kitty? We also look like our relatives. We look like Lizzy! Do you wish us gone, as well?"

Lydia was near to tears at the end of this speech, and Kitty was already there.

"Of course not, my dearest Lydia! I could never hate someone so beautiful and lively! You are my darling baby girl!"

Mary, while having a tendency towards sermonizing, was not without discernment. Something in her mother's wording and manner arrested her attention, causing a strength of feeling she had never before experienced.

"And, what about the rest of us? Do you hate me? What about Kitty? Neither of us has ever received such approbation from you as have Lydia and Jane. As a matter of fact, the only thing Jane has ever been praised for is her beauty. You have never once exclaimed over her accomplishments or her serenity."

Suddenly, Mary's own peace was shaken as anger took root in her heart at the expression on her mother's face. For even she, in her inexperience, could see that it was not what it should be.

"No, do not bother to respond. I can see that you have no maternal feelings for any of us." So saying, Mary arose from her seat and removed herself to her own bedchamber to cry and pray and ponder.

Jane looked helplessly at Lydia and Kitty. She was a serene young woman, always seeing only the best in those around her, but she knew right from wrong and was firm in her course of action when something was the latter. Her mother was wrong. It was not proper for a parent, in particular a mother, to feel as hers did about their own child. She also knew enough of Fitzwilliam and Mr. Darcy to know that they would be firm in their desire to stop all contact between her mother and her sister.

Mrs. Bennet loudly exclaimed, "Well, I never! It is clear to me that Mary has been spending too much time with that ungrateful sister of hers! Not love my own children! The idea …"

"Mama." Jane interrupted forcefully. "Please. It is as clear as the nose on your face that Mary and Lydia are correct. We, all of us, have only ever been to you a means to provide for you in your old age." She held up her hand as her mother began to protest. "I know that you love us, down deep in your heart, but you have not shown that love well at all. I am grateful today for Lydia's brashness, for it has opened a topic for discussion that would have never been addressed otherwise, but surely you see, Mama, that she is bold. She is loud and undisciplined. If you truly loved her, would you not censure her wild behavior? And Mary, who preaches to us all with little provocation. Do you think she has no feelings? Did it occur to you that she does what she does because she craves acceptance and love? No," she continued firmly. "You were wrong to speak to Lizzy the way you did, and you are wrong for not loving all your children equally.

"Lydia, Kitty, I think perhaps it would be best to leave our mother to ponder what we have spoken of today. Come, let us go to our rooms for a while."

As their mother watched, in shock that her gentlest and most tractable child would speak to her so, the remainder of her daughters quit the room. Without an audience, her attack of the vapors could not survive long, and soon Mrs. Bennet was left to her thoughts.

Chapter 8

The trip to Pemberley from Longbourn took two days, with the group staying overnight at inns twice. There were two carriages in their caravan: one containing the family, including Georgiana and her governess; and one containing the family's personal servants and enough luggage to carry a week's worth of clothing and other personal items. The wagon, which had been loaded with the remainder of the family's trunks and other items they were taking to Pemberley with them, had been sent ahead of them days ago.

Elizabeth's feelings about their travel were mixed. She enjoyed traveling very much. She had been to Pemberley before and had stayed in the same inns during those trips. Such was her personality that many of the innkeepers and their wives and servants remembered her. They were full of congratulations on her marriage and eager to be of service, making her time in their establishments easier.

However, this was the first time she had been to the estate since her marriage. She was eager to be there and see it from the point of view of a permanent resident and was thus very impatient with delays. Her family was kept in constant amusement at her exclamations and desire to hurry this maid or that footman or the coachman. In due time, her deepest desire was realized, as they pulled up to the magnificent house that was Pemberley.

Upon exiting the coach with assistance from Fitzwilliam, she was taken aback to see the entire household staff lined up on the steps to greet her. It took her so much by surprise, she stopped and stared for a moment before declaring, "All this pomp, for me? What can Mrs. Reynolds be thinking?"

"I think, Sweetheart, that she is welcoming the new mistress home."

"I am not the mistress yet, not really."

"No, I suppose not," Fitzwilliam replied with a tilt to his head, "but you have taken charge of Darcy House, and I know you expect to here, as well. Mrs. Reynolds is giving you your due." He lowered his voice before continuing. "You know there will be questions in the minds of the staff. They are too well trained to ask, but they will wonder at the speed of our union. Perhaps they will even be looking for evidence of a child. It is best, I think, that you are immediately recognized as a desired member of the household, and as the woman in charge of the home, in order to prevent problems in the future."

Elizabeth was astonished. It had never occurred to her that anyone here at Pemberley would question her reputation in such a way.

"You are right, as usual," she sighed quietly. "I had not thought of that. Well, let me assume my role now; lead on, my love."

She took hold of her husband's arm and allowed her father-in-law to present her to the assembled servants as the mistress of Pemberley. She greeted each one by name; many of them she knew from previous visits, but there were some who were new.

At the top of the steps was Mrs. Reynolds, Pemberley's housekeeper. Standing behind her were Jenny, Elizabeth's maid, and Mr. Reeves and Mr. Smith, valets to the Darcy men. Mrs.

Reynolds, delighted at the choice Master Fitzwilliam had made and not knowing that his marriage had been arranged, enthusiastically greeted the newest member of the family.

"Mrs. Darcy! How good it is to have you home!"

Elizabeth smiled. "Thank you, Mrs. Reynolds. I am happy to be here. Never in my wildest dreams on my previous visits did I think I would be allowed to live here for the rest of my life. I am delighted with the prospect!"

The housekeeper, whose hands were held together to prevent her from becoming too enthusiastic, squeezed them together even harder. "I am so pleased! Pemberley has needed a mistress for a long time; I am certain that you will be every bit as much a blessing to the estate as Lady Anne was. I have enjoyed seeing your growth from a child to a young woman. My excitement knows no bounds this day!"

Laughing, Elizabeth pulled her in for a quick hug, before letting go to whisper, "Thank you. I will endeavor to make you proud."

Mr. Darcy, seeing that the women were becoming emotional, took charge. "Mrs. Reynolds, I am sure that you ordered bathwater carried to our rooms when you first got word of our carriage entering the grounds. Perhaps we should go up and make use of it."

"Oh! Yes, sir; I apologize. I do indeed have baths awaiting each of you in your dressing rooms. There will be a meal ready to serve in an hour. As you requested in your letter, I have had Master Fitzwilliam's things moved from his old room to a suite." Turning to Elizabeth, she explained, "Mrs. Bishop wrote to me that you share accommodations at Darcy House, but Pemberley has more than enough room for you each to have a set of rooms for yourself. There is a suite that the master," she nodded to Mr. Darcy, "and Lady Anne shared when the old master was still alive. I have had that prepared for the two of you. You must let me know if it is not adequate."

Mr. Darcy assured her. "I am sure it will be. Thank you. I know we are all hungry and eager to rest and to refresh ourselves with Cook's fine fare. Thank you." With a smile to the housekeeper, he urged Georgiana inside, followed by Fitzwilliam with Elizabeth on his arm.

In short order, the family was settled into their baths. After, they all gathered in the family dining room, where they feasted on a celebratory dinner. Cook herself had come out from the kitchens to inform the master and his family that while Pemberley had celebrated Master Fitzwilliam's marriage while he was still in town, now that they were all at home, it would be celebrated again. Implied in this little speech was that Cook herself should have been the one to cook for the wedding breakfast, or at least an engagement dinner, and denied that, she was determined to make her approval of the match clear. Darcy chuckled to himself as she ended her speech, before he and his son and new daughter-in-law thanked her quite profusely. Once the cook had returned to the kitchen and the first course had been served, all the family members released their tightly held laughter.

"Father," Fitzwilliam began, "I do believe we have been chastised."

"I believe you are right." Darcy laughed. "Elizabeth, what say you? Do you feel properly welcomed now?"

"Indeed I do. Cook is usually so quiet. Who knew she could give such a speech?" Elizabeth's eyes twinkled merrily. It felt good to know she had the support of two of the most important of Pemberley's servants. She had always enjoyed a good rapport with both the housekeeper and the cook; that relationship would serve her well now.

~~~***~~~

As Elizabeth began to slowly learn and take over the tasks of mistress over the next few weeks, she would repeatedly speak of her relief to be on such good terms with those two women. For, as it turned out, there was much gossip about Elizabeth and Fitzwilliam among the younger and newer staff members. The gossip in turn became insolence on the part of a few. Mrs. Reynolds dealt with most of it, as it was her maids that were the problem, but Cook had one or two
~~~

of her own who disparaged the new mistress, as well. The day came, however, when Fitzwilliam heard of it, and Elizabeth was forced to take action herself.

One of the younger housemaids, a girl named Bertha, whose family had served the Darcys for generations, had heard rumors that the new Mrs. Darcy was not as high as her husband and his family. This gave her a disgust of her mistress and led to misbehavior on her part. She had already once or twice been warned by Mrs. Reynolds to cease and desist, but she ignored the warnings, not believing that she would be removed from her position. On this day, Mrs. Darcy asked her to bring a shawl to the blue sitting room, for it was a chilly morning and Elizabeth had forgotten to pick one up before descending the stairs to break her fast. Unbeknownst to Bertha, Fitzwilliam was to join her, and he entered the room behind the maid. When Bertha refused to "fetch and carry for a low-born woman like her," his anger was every bit as great as it had been the morning after her presentation ball. Soon, most of the household knew of it, because his fury was released in a loud and harsh peal rung over her head.

Young Bertha cowered in fear before Fitzwilliam and Elizabeth. Mrs. Reynolds and a footman rushed into the room to see what the matter was, and when the housekeeper caught sight of the maid and heard the words of the master's son, she sighed. There was nothing to be done. She had acted as she should; the rest was up to Bertha. It was apparent she had not heeded the words of wisdom imparted to her.

Elizabeth felt terrible that the situation had esca-lated to this. She knew how protective her husband was of her. She was aware that the staff was under her domain to deal with. She had given this particular maid the benefit of the doubt more than once, even though Mrs. Reynolds had suggested she be more forceful with her. And now here they were, in the exact position she had hoped to avoid. She stepped to her husband's side and took hold of his arm, distracting him from his tirade.

"How long has this been going on, Elizabeth?"

"She has been warned at least twice. I was hoping that would suffice. Please, let me handle this," she pleaded with him.

"She will not serve this house any longer. I am firm in this." He gave her a stern look, one she rarely received from him.

"Please, I understand now how wrong I was to be lenient. Mrs. Reynolds cautioned me against it," she said softly. "I am sorry, my love. I know how it upsets you when anyone is disrespectful to me. I am still learning to be mistress, and this has been a difficult lesson. I promise, I will let her go, but you must let me do it my way."

Fitzwilliam looked at her for a long moment, then stared at the maid for a longer moment, death in his eyes. Finally, she felt the muscles in his arm relax a bit. "Fine. I will let you deal with it. You know my opinion."

To Bertha, he tersely said, "Your family has faithfully served mine for years. Are there more of you who share the same opinions about Mrs. Darcy?"

"No, sir," she squeaked, terrified to be ad-dressed directly.

"I certainly hope not. Do not make the mistake of

thinking my wife will be lenient with you again. I have agreed to let her deal with you, but she is aware of my desires. At the very least, you will be gone from above stairs. You might think about attending the next hiring fair, for I guarantee you, if she allows you to remain, I will be sure to make your life as difficult as possible should I catch sight of you."

"Yes, sir!"

With that, he nodded to his wife, and strode from the room. He was surprised to see his father standing in the hallway, watching the goings-on. Mr. Darcy stayed his movement, silently encouraging him to observe how Elizabeth handled the situation.

Inside the room, Elizabeth cleared her throat. "I am sorry you feel the way you do about me. I can assure you that I am a gentleman's daughter. Mr. Darcy arranged my marriage to his son; I had nothing to do with it. He saved me when I was in danger, and I have since come to realize that I am deeply in love with him, as he is with me. Master Fitzwilliam wishes you gone from Pemberley, and I am already aware that Mr. Darcy will support my husband in his desires. You see, he has done it before, on numerous occasions. Therefore, as much as it pains me to do so, I must let you go. I cannot have servants who do not respect me in my employ. You have been given multiple opportunities to improve your behavior, yet it has only gotten worse. Mrs. Reynolds will accompany you to your room to gather your things, and she will pay you the wages you are due, then I will ask a footman to escort you from Pemberley property, and you are never to return. Am I clear? Do you understand what I am saying?"

"Yes, madam," the maid answered, in shock that she was truly being let go and escorted off the property like a common criminal. She opened her mouth to speak again, but before she got a word out, the housekeeper had her by the arm, almost dragging her into the hall and toward the servants' stairs.

Elizabeth remained within the room, her stomach rolling. She wrapped her arms around herself as she tried to hold in the tears that threatened. In the hallway, Darcy and Fitzwilliam had watched the entire event. When he saw her arms come up, Fitzwilliam strode into the room to wrap her in his embrace. He led her to a settee, sitting down, then settling her in his lap as the tears began to flow down her face.

"Oh, Fitzwilliam." She wailed into his neck, "I feel awful dismissing her like that!"

"Shh, my love, it had to be done; do not fret. You did well, and I am incredibly proud of you." He held her, rubbing her back and whispering words of love and support into her hair and her ear. Soon, her tears slowed. Once she had calmed, he led her up the stairs to their room, where he spent the remainder of the day showing her exactly how proud he was of her.

Below stairs, in the servants' hall, word quickly spread via the footman who had witnessed the spectacle that to disrespect Mrs. Darcy would result in termination. From that day onward, all the staff treated her with great deference, and in years to come would proclaim her the greatest mistress to ever rule Pemberley.

That evening at supper, Darcy suggested a picnic for the morrow, as a way to cheer Elizabeth. The entire family enthusiastically agreed.

<div align="center">~~~***~~~</div>

The day of the picnic dawned sunny, clear, and warm, to the delight of all. The morning was spent by the Darcy men in conference with the steward, Mr. Wickham. Elizabeth was similarly engaged with Mrs. Reynolds, reviewing menus and learning how Pemberley's manor house was run. Georgiana was, of course, occupied with lessons but greatly distracted by the activities to come when those lessons were completed. She was neither old enough nor mature enough to understand that the more she allowed thoughts of fun to distract her, the longer the lessons would actually take. This meant that they took far longer than they ought to have, to her dismay.

Finally, however, lessons and meetings were completed and the family gathered in the foyer to begin the trek to the chosen picnic grounds on the banks of the lake. The eagerness of the party to be out of doors, enjoying their play, was a tangible thing, spreading to the servants, who could not hold back their smiles. They, too, had been given the opportunity to picnic, thanks to their new mistress. They must do so in shifts, as they had to complete their work before they could participate, but for many it was the first chance in months they had to relax and ignore duty for a brief time. It raised Mrs. Darcy greatly in their esteem.

In a very few minutes, the family was seated in the open carriage, heading down the path to the lake. Behind followed a cart containing the picnic things and two footmen to set it all up. Elizabeth, who retained her appreciation for the ridiculous, laughed at the pomp involved in such a simple thing as a picnic. She was determined to teach her new family to relax their hold on propriety within the family party.

Elizabeth could not see it, as his head was turned away, but her Papa George smiled at her laughter. He and Fitzwilliam both could see how much more relaxed she was here, at the estate, than she had been in town, and it pleased them both greatly. Neither ever said anything to her about it, not wanting to add to her distress, but both understood the anxiety she had felt these last few months. For her to feel comfortable enough to laugh and tease about their methods of conducting a picnic was heartening.

In another few minutes, they were disembarking the carriage beside the lake, and the picnic was being laid out. They had chosen an area populated with tall, mature trees, shading it well and making the picnic more comfortable. The stream that fed the lake was nearby, and the constant sound of the water flowing, added to the sounds of the birds and buzzing of the insects, made it a very peaceful place. Father and son immediately baited their fishing hooks and cast out into the lake, while the sisters wandered off to a meadow that lay on the other side of the copse to gather wildflowers to decorate their "table." Once the servants had completed their work and returned to the manor, the family felt more comfortable in conversation. They teased and tormented each other with glee. For a time, Elizabeth and Georgiana joined Papa George and Fitzwilliam on the shore, talking quietly so as not to scare the fish away. After a while, hunger drove the entire family back to the blanket and the basket of food. Once it was consumed and the remains packed up, napping was the favored occupation. Finally, as the sun began to dip lower in the sky, they roused themselves to go back to the house. They would send the servants back out to clean up.

The day after the picnic brought with it neighbors,

knocking on the door, seeking to visit the family and introduce, or in some cases re-introduce, themselves to the new Mrs. Darcy. All were delighted with her; she was such a charming and witty young woman, and it was clear to all that Mr. Fitzwilliam Darcy was quite besotted with her.

Not all the neighbors had returned to the area, as of yet. The most prominent families were either still in London, or had travelled to visit relatives, taking advantage of the warm summer weather. In the end, it would be Christmastide before Elizabeth met them.

Chapter 9

"Fitzwilliam, I need to ride out to visit Mr. Barton today. Wickham has told me the roof of their house is leaking. I wish to see the damage my-self and ensure we get everything repaired. I would not put it past Barton to fail to report something, so as not to be a bother to anyone. Far too self-effacing, that one. It would not do for him to try to make those repairs with his own funds, not with four children to raise."

"You are correct. It would not do. I do not under-stand such behavior. Surely he would rather not use his own money to repair a home he does not own?"

"One would think not; however, he has done so in the past. I recall his father being a harsh man, always chastising his wife and children for being an impediment to him. He was not happy with his life, I think. Perhaps that is why his son is this way. At any rate, would you ride with me? I should like to get your opinion of the matter."

From the bedroom attached to the sitting room they were in, the gentlemen heard a series of harsh coughs. They looked at the door, then back to each other.

"If you do not mind, Father, I would much rather stay here and tend to Elizabeth. She woke in the night with that terrible cough and a sniffling nose. I am concerned about her."

"I had not realized she was ill! Certainly you should stay with her," Mr. Darcy replied. "Does she need the doctor? I can send him a note when I go downstairs."

"She does not show signs of a fever yet. I would

prefer waiting until that happens. You know how she can be if she feels she is being fussed over unnecessarily." Fitzwilliam rolled his eyes as his father chuckled.

"Indeed I do." He slapped his hands on his knees as he rose, adding, "Well, then, I will leave you to comfort and coddle your wife. But promise me that if she begins to become fevered, you will send for the physician."

Fitzwilliam had risen along with his parent. "I promise. I will see you upon your return. Please be careful."

Waving his son's concerns away, Darcy headed down the grand staircase and out the door to mount his waiting horse for the ride to the Barton farm.

He had not been gone an hour when the wind began to pick up and a light rain to fall. By the time he had thoroughly inspected the tenant house, spoken with both Mr. and Mrs. Barton, admired the children, and consulted with Mr. Wickham to give specific instructions as to repairs, the rain was coming down in sheets. Turning down an offer to wait out the storm with the Bartons, citing the closeness of Pemberley House to their own, he mounted once again and began the trek back. Moving more slowly than he had earlier, due to the reduced visibility caused by the weather, he turned his collar up in hopes of preventing any more rain from sliding down inside his coat. Suddenly, what had been a simple downpour became much more dangerous.

Darcy heard the thunder rolling in seconds before he saw the lightning. His horse moved uneasily beneath him, and every ounce of focus and skill he had was required to keep the animal under control. When the next blast of thunder sounded loudly in his ears followed by an even closer crack of lightning, the horse began to rear. Darcy fought to regain the upper hand, but when it began to buck, he lost his seat, landing on his back with a thud, his head slamming into the hard-packed earth of the path.

Out of breath and woozy, he laid on the ground for a few minutes, rain soaking and pooling around him. After a few minutes, he tried to rise. Pain in his leg and head stopped him, and he lay back down in the hopes it would recede once again. Next he tried to peer through the storm to locate his horse, but was unsuccessful. Hopefully, the silly thing returned to the stables, he thought. That one will need some additional training.

He attempted to move once or twice more before giving up. He knew an alarm would be raised if his horse appeared without him. Even if it remained nearby, when he failed to come to supper, Fitzwilliam would know something was wrong. He's a good boy. I am so glad he did not fight me about Elizabeth. She was just what he needed. Darcy's thoughts continued on until, exhausted and in pain, his unconscious took over and allowed his mind to rest.

~~~***~~~

At the house, his son was trying to entice his wife to take some tea laced with honey for her throat. She had not eaten much that day, and Fitzwilliam was anxious that she take some nourishment, even if it was of the liquid variety. He had begun to threaten her with honey-laced Scottish whiskey if she did not take the tea. Stubborn woman that she was, Elizabeth argued with him, which, of course, made her throat hurt worse.

"Sweetheart, did you not just recently chastise
~~~

Georgiana for being so impatient for her lessons to be complete so she could attend our picnic? And did you not tell her that the quicker she worked, the sooner she could play?" At her nod and before she could begin to speak, he continued. "Do you not see the similarity in your situations? The quicker you drink this tea, the sooner I will stop fussing at you about it and threatening you with stronger remedies." He hid a smirk at the roll of her eyes and twitch of her head. "Drink this tea, my love, and I shall leave you be about it for a few hours."

With a loud sigh, followed by another harsh bout of coughing, Elizabeth drank the tea. It did feel good on her throat, though she was not about to tell her husband that. He was correct entirely too often; she must do her best to ensure his understanding that this was not allowed. She opened her mouth to say so when a knock came upon the dressing room door.

Entering at Fitzwilliam's bidding was his valet. "Pardon me, sir. I have an urgent message for you." He threw a quick glance at the mistress, telling his master without words that it was serious and that perhaps she did not need to hear.

Turning to his wife, Fitzwilliam stroked her face, saying, "Let me go listen to what Smith has to say. I shall return shortly." He leaned toward her, giving her a quick kiss on the forehead, then stood and left the room, gesturing for his valet to follow him. Upon gaining his dressing room and shutting the door behind them, he asked, "What is it?"

"Sir, word has just come from the stables. Your father's horse has returned without him. Mr. Wickham has been notified, and search parties are being organized. Wickham felt you would wish to take part. I was not as certain, knowing Mrs. Darcy to be ill, but I promised to tell you straight away."

Fitzwilliam was, for a few seconds, panic-stricken. He looked to the window, seeing the rain beating on the glass and the lightning illuminating the sky, and hearing the accompanying thunder. "I should have gone with him," he muttered, guilt winding its way into his heart. Now was not the time for recriminations, however, so he shoved his feelings aside and focused on those actions that urgently needed to be taken.

To Smith he said, "Yes, I wish to help with the search. Give me time to inform Mrs. Darcy and change my clothes and I will be down. Send word to the physician in Lambton that he may be needed." His eyes slid once more to the window, thoughts of his father out in the rain, possibly hurt, causing dread in his heart. "Hopefully we find him right away. He only went to the Bartons'. Also, please send Mrs.

Darcy's maid up to sit with her. She is still very ill, and I do not like to leave her alone."

"Yes, sir. Is there anything else? Shall I have more tea sent up for the mistress?"

"She has just now taken a cup; perhaps in an hour or so, she might take some soup. Please see to that, as well. Thank you, Smith."

Knowing he was now dismissed, the valet left to quickly lay out riding clothes for Master Fitzwilliam before seeing to the other tasks laid before him.

After dismissing Mr. Smith, Fitzwilliam went back into the bedchamber to apprise his wife of the situation. Elizabeth loved her father-in-law deeply, and, despite the valet's reservations about it, would be resentful if left unaware and the worst happened. He quickly related to her the facts as he knew them before informing her that he intended to join the search. She had no objections;

instead she was quite insistent that he do so. He would not leave, however, without gaining her promise to stay abed, drink the tea and honey, and eat some soup when it was sent up. Her pledge made, Fitzwilliam hurried to his dressing room to change before going downstairs and out to the stables, where the search parties were being organized.

~~~***~~~

It was not above an hour later when the master of Pemberley was found unconscious. The grooms who found him fired the gun they carried to alert the remaining searchers and then set to work. One evaluated the master and made him comfortable while the other rode back to the stables to get a wagon. Soon everyone involved had gathered around him to help load him into the cart. Fitzwilliam was terrified to see his father so lifeless on the ground. He urged his workers
~~~

to move faster, sending one ahead to the house to alert Mrs. Reynolds of their coming.

Not soon enough to please him, the men were carrying his father into Pemberley House and up the stairs to his chambers. Fitzwilliam was shouting orders right and left, commanding the waiting doctor to follow him upstairs, and sending a maid to inform his wife that they were returned.

Mr. Reeves, his father's valet, was waiting in his room to wait on Mr. Darcy, and help Fitzwilliam and the doctor remove his master's soaked clothing. While the doctor conducted his examination with Reeves' assistance, Fitzwilliam walked down the hall to change his own attire. Smith was waiting for him, with warm water in the ewer for washing and a dry set of breeches, shirt, waistcoat, and tailcoat. Having seen to his own needs and aware that the doctor required more time, Fitzwilliam went into the bedroom he shared with his wife, dismissing her maid with a glance.

"Fitzwilliam! They told me you had returned; how is Papa George? Is he well? The maid knew no details, and Jenny forced me to keep my promise to you to stay abed. Sometimes I do not know who is mistress, she or I," she huffed.

As she had been speaking, her husband had settled on the bed beside her, leaning against the headboard. Now he gathered her close, hoping to soothe her fears rather than increase them. "Jenny wants to keep her mistress well, thereby making her mistress' husband happy and her employment secure." He chuckled. "She does not lack in intelligence. Besides, did you not make me a solemn promise to stay in bed and eat some soup and rest so I could assist in the search for Papa without the added distraction of worrying about you?"

Another huff from his wife was followed by, "You know I did. Still, it would not have gone amiss for me to be up to assist when Papa George was brought into the house."

"We managed quite well, my love. You need to take care of yourself even more now, because he may require some nursing." He sighed, hating to have to tell her, "He was unconscious, Sweetheart. I suspect he was thrown from his horse and hit his head. That path is quite hard, even in wet weather such as this. There is a base of rock under a top layer of dirt." He paused, tightening his hold on her as if he could shield her from the words he must say. "I also believe his leg is broken. The doctor is with him now. We will know nothing more until his examination is complete."

Elizabeth, whose worry was only slightly eased with the knowledge that her beloved father-in-law was in the house and not out in the storm, quietly spoke. "I feel so guilty. If I had not been ill, you would not have needed to stay with me. You would have been with him, and he would not have lain out in the rain for who knows how long. I am sorry!" With that, she began sobbing into Fitzwilliam's shoulder.

"Shhh, Sweetheart. Shhhh. I feel guilt, as well. However, it was my choice to stay with you. Mine," he declared, lifting her face with his hand under her chin. "I could have gone with him, but I chose you. I will always choose you," he finished, hovering over her lips until the words faded away, then covering them with his own. Their kiss was long and sweet, feeling as though it would never end. When they needed to catch their breath, he moved his hand from her chin, pushing her head into his body and laying his cheek on it. They remained in this comforting embrace for a long time, each gaining strength from the other's presence and reassurance from the other's touch. Too soon, their interlude was interrupted by a knock on the door.

"Come."

Smith appeared just inside the room, eyes averted from the bed. "The doctor is finished treating the master and asks to speak with you, sir."

"Thank you, Smith; I shall be down shortly. Please put him in my father's study and have refreshments sent in to him."

Smith nodded his acknowledgement and left to carry out his instructions.

With a final cuddle and kiss, Fitzwilliam rose from the bed, tucked his wife back in, and descended the stairs to hear what the doctor had to say. He paused at the door, hand on the latch, to mentally prepare himself for whatever he might hear. Taking a deep breath, he opened the panel and stepped into the room.

"Mr. Stone, thank you for coming so late and in such terrible weather. How is my father?"

"He is still unconscious; he has a lump on the back of his head that I believe indicates the cause. He was thrown from his horse, I understand?" At Fitzwilliam's nod, he continued. "I would guess he hit his head rather forcefully on the ground when he fell. Such injuries are always tricky. One never knows what the end result will be; he could wake in a few hours or never awaken again. If he does …"

"When he does."

The doctor cleared his throat. "Indeed. When he does." He nodded to Fitzwilliam. "He could be perfectly normal or be left with a permanent injury. We know so little of these things; only time will tell."

Fitzwilliam nodded. "And, is that his only injury?"

"His leg is broken, just above his ankle. I have set the bone and splinted it. Should he wake, he will need to remain abed for two months. He has no other injuries that I can see; however, fever is always a risk. Someone must sit with him constantly to monitor him."

"Of course." Glancing out the window, Fitzwilliam said, "The storm continues to rage. May I offer you accommodations for the night?"

"Thank you, Mr. Darcy; I accept your offer with appreciation. I will look in on your father again before I retire. And, perhaps a visit to Mrs. Darcy might not be amiss? I gathered from your staff that she has been ill today?"

"She has. No fever as of yet, but a cough and sore throat. It would ease my mind if you would examine her, though I must warn you that she is not an easy patient. Stubborn, that one," he replied with a twinkle in his eye and his lips twisted into a smirk.

Laughing, the doctor arose, saying, "Stubborn, eh? Been giving you a hard time, has she? She is a fiery one!"

Fitzwilliam joined in the laughter as he led the physician into the hall. Gesturing to the footman on duty, he requested the doctor be shown to a room before walking up to his father's bedchamber. As he approached the bed, he indicated to Reeves that he should take some time to rest himself. He stood beside his father, observing him, until he heard the door shut as the other man's personal servant left the room. Only then did he sit, pulling the chair beside the bed as near as he could get it. His father's hand lay close, and he held it in both of his, leaning over as near as he could to whisper, "Come back to us, Papa. We need you, all of us. I need you! I am not prepared to run Pemberley alone; my education is incomplete. I am sorry that I stayed behind today. I should have been with you; please, forgive me!"

Quietly, he sobbed at his father's bedside. Despite his words to Elizabeth and hers to him, the guilt he felt was tremendous. Yet, he knew that, had he accompanied his father this day and Elizabeth took a turn for the worst, he would feel guilty for that, as well. He was correct when he told his beloved wife that he chose to stay with her. He could easily have left her, but one thing his father had stressed to him shortly after his marriage was that his priority must now be his wife. Not his father or his sister, not his friends or his business, but his wife. A true gentleman kept his priorities in order: God, then family, then business; he also left his mother and father and cleaved to his spouse. As he sat there, crying and contemplating all these things, he prayed. He prayed for his father's restoration to health, forgiveness for his own confusion, and for peace about his decision and its aftermath. Soon, Reeves returned, and Fitzwilliam went back to his chambers to check on Elizabeth.

<div align="center">~~~***~~~</div>

Once her husband had left to talk with the doctor, Elizabeth realized that Georgiana might not know about her father's accident. She thought for a while, not knowing how much the girl needed to know, but in the end, decided honesty was best. She knew that she herself, at Georgiana's age, would have insisted on having all the facts. It was much better to be aware of events and have time to prepare than to be taken by surprise should the worst happen. Therefore, she asked her maid to have her sister sent in to her. Once Georgiana arrived and settled on the bed with her, she used the gentlest terms possible to explain that Papa George had an accident, that Fitzwilliam had gone down to speak to the doctor, and that all she knew of his condition was that he was not awake.

Georgiana was frightened by this information, asking many questions, most of which Elizabeth did not have answers for. Finally, she simply asked to stay there, with her sister, and wait her brother's return, a request Elizabeth was glad to grant. So it was that Fitzwilliam entered the bedchamber he shared with his wife, to find his sister cuddled beside her, held tight in her embrace.

Smiling at the sight they made, he settled on the bed on his wife's other side. "Georgiana, I assume by your presence here, you are aware of Papa's accident?"

Elizabeth reached for his hand. "I am sorry, my darling. I should have consulted you before telling her, but I know that were I in her shoes, I would not want to be left in the dark about such an incident."

He kissed her hair. "I agree. I apologize, Sister, for not thinking to inform you myself."

"It is well, Brother. I am glad my sister told me, but I understand that you had responsibilities to Papa that needed to be taken care of first. How is he?" Georgiana's question was tentatively put forward, her brow creased.

"He is still unconscious. It appears he struck his head rather forcefully on the ground when his horse threw him; he has a large lump on the back of it. He has bruises, of course, and a broken leg. He will need us to take turns sitting with him; do you think you will be able to do that, or will it upset you too much?"

"I should like to try," Georgiana said with determination. "Part of becoming a lady and mistress of a house is taking care of others, is it not?" She looked to her brother and sister in turn. When both had nodded their agreement, she continued. "Then, since I want to learn to be a good mistress, I think my education should begin now. I also desperately want to be near Papa and talk to him and assure him that I need him."

Seeing that she had turned back into the little girl she still was, Fitzwilliam agreed. "Why do I not take you down now to visit him for a few minutes? Tomorrow, we can set a schedule of visits around your lessons. You must not neglect those just because Papa is abed. You know that is what he would tell you."

Georgiana sighed. "Lessons. Yes, Brother, I can hear Papa saying those exact words. Apparently, nothing but death comes between a young lady and her lessons." Shaking her head, she left the room, her brother following. Behind her, Fitzwilliam and Elizabeth did all they could to hold in their laughter, but once he had shut the wooden panel after entering the hall, Elizabeth could no longer control hers. It rang out through the door and the hallway and into his ears, causing him to smile and cough to cover his own chuckle.

~~~***~~~

That night, as the couple prepared for bed, they
~~~

discussed their sister's visit to her father.

"She was distraught; it was plain to see." Fitzwilliam's voice rang with pride for Georgiana. "Yet, she worked hard to control herself. There was no dramatic throwing herself across him on the bed. She sat beside him, holding his hand and talking to him for a good quarter hour. I was quite amused at the peevishness in her voice as she assured him that I was well in control of things, and that I had promised her that her education would continue while he was laid up. Truly, my love, it was a struggle to pretend I did not hear and was not amused by her words."

Laughing, his wife responded, "I know, darling. We really should not encourage such behavior, but she is still very young. She will learn. And I confess to enjoying her outspokenness."

"Indeed." Though she could not see his face, Elizabeth could hear the smile in her Fitzwilliam's voice.

"Did she assure him of her love and devotion? She was quite distressed earlier at the thought of never saying those words to him again. She asked if I thought he would hear if she told him while he was not yet awake. I told her I did not know, but it would not hurt to say them, regardless."

"I am glad you did. You handled her very well, my love. Thank you for taking care of that for me. I cannot imagine how I would have alone. It is just one more reason for me to be grateful for my father's interference in my love life."

"Love life! What love life? I know for a fact that you never looked at a woman but to find fault before you married me," she teased.

Fitzwilliam laughed, "Once again, you are correct, my dear little wife." He paused to give her a kiss, then climbed into the bed with her and gathered her close. "That is because none were you."

"Such a flatterer you are, Mr. Darcy! Do you think those pretty words will earn you a reward of some sort?"

With a huge smile at her teasing flirt, he responded, "I do indeed, my love," before kissing her passionately and demonstrating just what kind of reward he expected.

<div align="center">~~~***~~~</div>

Mr. Darcy awakened late the next morning. With him at the time was the doctor, who was in the midst of examining him again, and Fitzwilliam. Hovering behind them was Mr. Reeves. Darcy moaned at the pain the doctor's poking produced, not to mention that caused by the bright light. He felt as though he had been hit by a runaway team of horses. After asking for a drink of water, he inquired of his son, "What happened?"

Holding tightly to his father's hand, Fitzwilliam responded. "Your horse threw you, we believe. He appeared at the stables without you late yesterday afternoon, in the height of the storm. Wickham immediately organized a search, and thankfully you were found quickly."

"He threw me? I do not remember. What was I doing out in bad weather?"

"You had gone to the Bartons' house to inspect for repairs. Do you remember that?"

Darcy closed his eyes tightly and tried to think. In his mind's eye, he could see himself speaking to his steward and the tenant in question.

"Yes, I believe I do, but I think Wickham was with me. Did he not leave with me also?"

"I asked him that, Father. After you left Barton's,

Wickham rode to the Milton house to deal with a problem there. He returned another way. He expected you to already be at home when he got back, but instead found the grooms and coachmen in an uproar. I believe he feels a fair amount of guilt, as do Elizabeth and I, for your accident. I have told him, though, that none of us could have expected a Pemberley-trained animal to spook as yours apparently did."

"None of you are to feel guilty. My accident was my own fault. From what I am hearing, I knowingly went out into a storm. I should have taken refuge at Barton's. I am certain they would have welcomed me to stay."

"Yes, sir. Wickham told me they offered but that you were eager to return home." He paused, then added, "I am sorry that I did not accompany you myself. I know I chose rightly to stay with my wife, and I was not able to be in both places at once, but I cannot help thinking that had I gone with you, you would not have lain in the rain as you did for hours before we found you." By now, Fitzwilliam was up, pacing the room as he always did when agitated.

"Son, come." Darcy gestured to the open spot on the bed beside him. "Sit down here with me. My head aches enough without watching you wear holes in the floor. I am going to cast my accounts all over this bed if I have to see it much longer."

Immediately, Fitzwilliam stopped walking and sat on the bed where his father indicated. "I am sorry, sir. I was not thinking properly."

"Do not fret. I am fine, or I will be. Son, I meant it when I said no one should feel guilty for my accident. I alone am responsible for the actions that led to it. And, I never want to hear you express regret for putting the wife of your heart first in your life. You know what you were taught about being a gentleman; I have no need of repeating it. You made the correct choice. Make sure Elizabeth understands this, as well. I know her well enough to know she will take the blame on her small shoulders if she can. You must not allow her."

"I will not." Fitzwilliam could see his father was tiring. "I will go now and let you rest. I am sure Georgiana would like to see you again, now that you are awake; I will bring her in later. I love you, Papa."

"Thank you, Son; I love you, too." Darcy fell asleep as his son left the room.

Chapter 10

With the care and attention of his family and servants, Darcy made a rapid recovery. Within a couple of weeks, the headaches caused by his head injury had all but disappeared, and his bruises faded. His memory of the accident was slow to return, and his broken ankle took the rest of the summer to mend, but he was soon eager to return to the helm and take back the running of the estate from Fitzwilliam. His children, with support from the doctor, insisted he do so from his bed. Reluctantly, he gave in.

During this time of recuperation for the master of Pemberley, visits between the residents and the neighbors came to a halt. Letters were sent back and forth between the families, but no one wished to intrude on them when the master was ill. Nor were Fitzwilliam and Elizabeth in any mood to go around the neighborhood as though nothing were the matter. They were far too busy with estate and nursing duties.

Added to their burden was the desire to be strong for each other, and for each to absolve the other of any responsibility for Darcy's accident. Both repeatedly heard his words against such feelings; each repeated them to the other, sometimes daily, yet they both were aware of their own guilt. Neither could really see the truth in their father's words in relation to their own decisions; yet, they could clearly comprehend it for their spouse. Oddly enough, it was this constant holding each other up, this frequency of speaking a lack of guilt over each other that eventually began to turn their feelings. First convincing each other of their own innocence in the matter, they began turning their thoughts and words of forgiveness inward. Once that happened, they began to realize that their father was correct, and were able to forgive themselves.

~~~***~~~

One of the duties the young couple took on was visits to tenants. While it was a task Elizabeth would have taken over eventually, no one had planned on it being forced upon her so soon. Still, the visits would have to be made, and she was eager to begin. She was acquainted with a few of those who lived closer to the manor house, though she had never met the ones who lived further out. Fitzwilliam insisted on making the first round of visits with her, both for her support and to see for himself what the situation of each family was.

As they rode in her husband's curricle out to the
~~~

first family on the list, Elizabeth realized just how eager she was. She considered her reasons and realized that she had nothing to fear from any of the people she was about to meet. She was the mistress of Pemberley. She had protection in the form of her father and husband, she was married and thus not to be pursued, and her status was higher than theirs, all of which meant she would receive deference and respect rather than snobbery and abuse. Added to the situation – this was not a London ballroom or the drawing room of a peer – her comfort level was the highest it had been outside of home for a long time. She smiled widely. Fitzwilliam, catching sight of the twinkle in her eye, naturally enquired as to the reason. Elizabeth happily shared her thoughts with him.

"I am not dreading these visits, and I asked myself why. I concluded I have no reason to, and I am ecstatic to be unafraid."

"I am glad to hear it. You, Mistress, are going to be loved by all who meet you today." He leaned over to punctuate his words with a quick kiss to his wife's enticing smile.

Elizabeth responded by holding his arm tighter, cuddling as close to him as she dared in such a public place. This, combined with her words, inspired her adoring spouse to pull the curricle off the road and into a wide path in the trees. When he was sure they were far enough from the road so as not to be seen, he stopped the horses and turned to his wife, pulling her into his arms. They kissed deeply, expressing their pleasure in each other's company the best way they knew how. Soon enough, hands began to wander and desire to race, but they kept their heads about them and desisted before they went too far. The day promised to be a long one, and they wanted to get as many farms in as they could before it got too late. Eventually, Fitzwilliam got the equipage turned around again and they were back on the road toward the farms.

They stopped to see the Bartons first. Mr. and Mrs. Barton were relieved to hear from Master Fitzwilliam's own lips that Mr. Darcy was doing well.

"We begged him to stay, sir. That rain was coming down in buckets! The missus offered him supper, even. He was insistent he was going home." Mr. Barton shook his head at the memory, even as his wife nodded hers in agreement.

Elizabeth was quick to reassure them. "We are so grateful that you offered," she began earnestly. "Mr. Darcy, as you have learned, is quite willful when he is of a mind to be. You did the best you could, and I assure you, none of us hold it against you."

"Thank ye, Mrs. Darcy," a relieved Mrs. Barton responded. "The Darcys have always been the best family to work for. And we …" She reached to tuck her hand into Mr. Barton's elbow. "Believe what we learned at church, to do to others what we would have done to us. Mr. Darcy takes good care of his tenants. It is an honor and a pleasure to take care of his family in return, when the need arises."

Soon after this exchange, Fitzwilliam and Elizabeth were on their way to the next farm. Every family was eager for first-hand news of the master, for even though Wickham kept them updated, the words meant more coming from the family itself.

At the end of the day, they had made brief visits to almost all who leased farmland from Pemberley. Elizabeth's joy in the visits was plain to see, and the families rejoiced that such a warm and outgoing young woman was now mistress. Her charm and wit were a stark contrast to her husband's, but they could see the warmth and pride in his eyes when he looked upon her. The future of the estate looked brighter, in the tenants' eyes, and was cause for celebration.

With that in mind, Fitzwilliam pulled back into the hidden spot they had made use of earlier in the day. Their passion had been quietly simmering through all the calls, and neither was prepared to wait until nightfall for satisfaction. This time, when they returned to the main road, both were glowing and slightly disheveled.

~~~***~~~

Eventually, the elder Darcy was out of bed and using canes to get around. It was now late September, and preparations for the harvest were being made. The days were still rather hot, and
~~~

the family enjoyed time spent out of doors as often as their schedules allowed. During one of these picnics, Darcy brought something up to Elizabeth that he was sure the housekeeper had already addressed, or was about to.

"Elizabeth," he began, "I do not remember your family ever visiting in the autumn, but one of the traditions that my wife always organized was a harvest festival for the tenants and workers. Has Mrs. Reynolds said anything to you about it?"

"No, she has not, not yet. What goes on during this festival?"

"Mainly, it is a feast to which all of Pemberley is invited. I remember Anne organizing activities, though. There were games for the children, especially, and I recall activities for the adults, as well."

Fitzwilliam interjected, "I remember you and Uncle

Henry taking part in a footrace one year."

"Yes, and one year we raced Pemberley's horses." Darcy smiled fondly. The memories were as vivid today as they had been ten years ago on the day his wonderful wife had passed away.

Turning his focus back to Elizabeth, he continued. "Anne had a great talent for organizing gatherings of all kinds. I am sure if you asked some of the older tenants, they would be full of stories of our festivals then."

Smiling at him, Elizabeth agreed. "Perhaps I will do just that. Thank you for sharing this with me. I will ask Mrs. Reynolds tomorrow; I know she will have journals of previous festivals, as she has kept detailed descriptions of every event Pemberley has ever held, it seems."

The family shared a laugh, as it was a fair depiction of the housekeeper's great attention to detail.

The next morning, during their meeting, Elizabeth did ask Mrs. Reynolds, who did have several journals containing accounts of previous harvest festivals. The two began planning for this year's party to be held at the end of October, once the remaining crops had been harvested.

~~~***~~~

Hearing a knock on the open door to her sitting room, Elizabeth looked up. There stood a footman looking very much as though he wished to speak to her.

"Come in, Joshua. How may I help you?"

Clearing his throat and bowing to her, he began, "Mrs. Darcy, your presence is requested in the master's study."

Elizabeth was surprised. She wondered what
~~~

possible need for her Papa George could have. Her thoughts quickly turned to her husband, and she blushed. Surely he could not be requesting a private rendezvous in his father's study! Before her mind wandered any further, she thanked Joshua and dismissed him to return to his duties.

When she arrived at the study door, she was astonished to hear her newest sister's voice. She knocked with her hand on the latch, jumping back when it opened on its own. Standing on the other side, head peeking around to see who requested entrance, was Fitzwilliam. The relief on his face was almost comical, but she held back her smile until she could ascertain what was distressing him so.

"Elizabeth, I am so glad you responded so promptly!" her husband exclaimed. He reached for her hand, almost pulling her into the room before shutting the door again.

"What is the problem?" She looked into each face. She could see frustration in the male countenances and stubborn anger in the female one.

Georgiana burst out, "I will not go. You cannot make me!"

"Go where, dearest?"

Darcy cleared his throat. "I have just informed Georgiana that she is to go to school in the fall, following the harvest festival."

Fitzwilliam added, "She refuses to attend. Elizabeth, you have told me many times of your desire to be educated and your disappointment when your request was refused. Please, will you not speak to her? See if you can change her mind. Where this stubbornness and outright rudeness has come from, I do not know."

"Fitzwilliam …"

"I apologize, Father. I should not have questioned your parenting."

Elizabeth laughed. "You do not know where her bull-headedness came from? Have you looked in the mirror recently? It is a family trait!"

Her husband turned red, and her father-in-law chuckled. He had been accused of that fault many times by his beloved Anne and was well-aware of the arguments Fitzwilliam and Elizabeth had gotten into, in large part due to the refusal of one or the other – or sometimes both – to see any other point of view but their own. Fitzwilliam was also recalling a couple of those arguments. Mostly the ones he had lost. He covered his embarrassment by returning the discussion to its topic.

"We were discussing my sister and her education."

Smirking, she replied, "Yes, my darling, we were." Turning to her sister, she sat down beside her and took her hand. She asked, "Do you comprehend the great honor you are receiving to be able to go to school, to learn in a formal manner? Fitzwilliam is correct. I have told him many times how I begged my father to send me. I pleaded and made vows and promises, but to no avail. There was not money for it, I was told. 'I can teach you just as well,' he said. And then there was my mother, who did not believe a girl child should have any education at all beyond basic reading and doing sums. But I craved books. I wanted to devour every bit of knowledge I could. It is well that I had that desire, as I was forced to educate myself. Georgiana, I beg you, do not throw this opportunity away! You will come to regret it later if you do. It can be nothing but a blessing to you, truly!"

"But I do not want to leave you and Fitzwilliam and Papa! I would be in London, so far away from you, all alone!" Georgiana wailed, truly distressed at the idea.

"You will have your Matlock relations right there in town, dearest. Uncle Henry's duties in Parliament will keep them there even after we have returned to Pemberley. And you will come home for Christmas; will she not, Papa George?" Elizabeth asked as she turned from her sister to her father.

"Indeed she will. I will go to town myself to retrieve her. Georgiana, I would never leave you friendless, especially not on holidays. You will always come home when school is not in session. Your aunt and uncle, as well as Elizabeth's aunt and uncle, are available to you whenever you need them. I have authorized both to speak for me should the need arise.

"You are a Darcy, and one day you will come out and be an adult woman. You will need to have all manner of accomplishments. There is much you can learn from Elizabeth, but there is more you will only hear about at school. You will make connections there, as well; friends of your own. Fitzwilliam went to school when he was about your age. It is expected of one of our status."

"I will not have to stay at school all the time?"

"Well, when it is in session, you will. It is a boarding school; you will sleep there and eat your meals and everything as though you were here. However, when school is out for holidays and breaks, you will come home, to Pemberley if we are here, or to Darcy House if we are in town. If you study hard, perhaps I might even bring you home for a Saturday night now and then, or maybe a whole weekend. But you must work hard," he finished sternly.

"Georgie, has that been your concern, that you would be stranded at the school and not see us again for the entire term?" Elizabeth asked.

Georgiana began to cry. "Yes! I do not want to leave you for months and months. I finally have a sister, and you want me to leave. Our family is complete, for the first time I can remember. If I go to school, I will never see you, not for a long time!"

Elizabeth held her, looking over her head at her men, who looked abashed; it had occurred to neither of them to ask. They had assumed she was simply being obstinate.

"Will you go, dearest, given the reassurance that you will see us again soon?"

Georgiana sniffed. "Yes, I will go." She looked up, glaring at her father. "But you must promise me that you will not leave me there."

Relieved, Darcy repeated his assurances. After relaying more details, the entire family retreated to their rooms to recover from the emotional conversation.

"My love, I do not know what Father and I would have done without you today. Thank you for seeing what we did not."

Elizabeth smiled. "I think you would have figured it out sooner or later. But I am happy to have so quickly and easily restored harmony to us all." She stood up on her toes to kiss her husband, who wrapped her tightly in his embrace. It was not until dinner was about to be served, hours later, that the couple made it down the stairs again.

~~~***~~~

When the day of the harvest celebration arrived,
~~~

the entire estate expressed their delight. Elizabeth had reinstated some of Lady Anne's favorite events, many of which had not been part of the festival since her death. Each of the Darcy family members played a part. Georgiana led the games for the children, Fitzwilliam and Elizabeth took charge of the activities for the adults – and participated in a few, to the delight of the tenants and workers – and the estate's master oversaw the horse race. A huge feast was laid out early in the afternoon for all to enjoy, followed by dancing in the evening and fireworks at dusk. At some point during the party, every attendee made their way to Mr. Darcy and his family to thank them and express their appreciation.

"This is the best estate in all of England to work for, sir. I remind my boys of that daily," effused Mr. Mitchell, one of the more prosperous of the tenants.

"Thank you, Mitchell. We are happy to have you. Without tenants and workers like you, who put in a good, solid days' work, Pemberley would be nothing."

"Thank ye, sir. Mrs.," he tugged at his forelock as he bowed, taking his leave of the couple.

Elizabeth sighed. "What a lovely day this has been. It was such a joy to see everyone enjoying themselves!"

"It is all due to you, my love. You have set a high standard for future celebrations, you know."

"Yes, but I know they all work so hard for us. It is the least I could do for them."

"Indeed." Fitzwilliam squeezed the hand that lay on his arm, fingers intertwined with his.

Finally, after the last of the fireworks faded into black, the families began gathering together to return to their homes. When all was quiet, the Darcys followed suit.

<p align="center">~~~***~~~</p>

The next day, Darcy and Georgiana headed off to London to enroll her in school. Fitzwilliam and Elizabeth considered going with them for the Little Season, but instead decided to stay at Pemberley. Being well into autumn, the days were cooler, but that did not stop them from having a final picnic. So, after waving off their father and sister, the pair climbed into Fitzwilliam's curricle, picnic basket stowed at their feet, and drove off to their favorite, secluded glen for an afternoon of talk, sleep, and love.

Chapter 11

Elizabeth walked the hallways of Pemberley, taking her daily exercise. In good weather she liked to walk outside, wandering the paths of the estate for hours. This close to Christmas, however, it was entirely too cold and her husband, with the backing of his father, had forbid her such activity. Elizabeth had eventually caved in to the pressure to give up one of her favorite things to do; in its place, she insisted on indoor strolls. Though "stroll" might be a misnomer, for Elizabeth always walked rather briskly. She enjoyed physical activity and was not about to let the frigid Derbyshire winter put a stop to it.

As she strode along, Elizabeth reflected on the past year, ticking items and events off in her head. She had survived her first season in London. She had taken over the duties of mistress of this wonderful estate as well as tenant visits, and helped nurse her father-in-law back to health after his accident. She had organized the best harvest festival Pemberley had seen in years and had convinced her sister to go to school. It has been a busy, fulfilling, and challenging year, she thought.

~~~***~~~

When Georgiana had been sent off to the exclusive boarding school chosen for her in London in the autumn, she still had not wanted to go, but she bravely and stoically entered the institution that first day. To her delight and surprise, she enjoyed her classes, liked her teachers, and made some very good friends amongst her fellow students. Now she was home and had regaled Elizabeth with story after story of her les-
~~~

sons, teachers, and new friends. It was good to have her with them again, in Elizabeth's opinion. She had missed her sister greatly while she was away, just as she missed the four sisters she had grown up with.

Coming to the end of her walk, Elizabeth turned her thoughts to her husband. As she headed towards his father's study, she smiled, thinking of all the ways he was so perfect for her. The two of them had known each other for years before marrying. They shared many of the same tastes in books, music, and entertainment. Both loved the theater and Shakespeare. Fitzwilliam, being more sedate in nature than Elizabeth, preferred histories and tragedies. Elizabeth, being livelier and more outgoing, preferred comedies. That is not to say that she did not read everything she could get her hands on. She did. The couple had spent many an evening curled up together in the library or their private sitting room reading to themselves and to each other.

They had done more than read together in eight months since their marriage, of course. Fitzwilliam had taught her to ride as a child, and they had traversed the entire estate and a large part of Mayfair in London on horseback. They had visited the theater many times, and had attended several balls and dinners. They engaged each other in stimulating conversation; so quick was their repartee that they often left their listeners in a state of confusion. Never had they had a dull moment.

Of course, it had not all been a bed of roses. Both were headstrong and stubborn. More than once in their youths had they been reprimanded by their elders for arguing. They had promised upon becoming engaged to respect each other, though, and had decided early on to never go to bed angry. They were learning to talk to each other and that communication was the key to a happy marriage. Arguments always seemed to happen when they did not explain themselves fully.

Soon, Elizabeth arrived at the room she had been seeking and entered without thought. Both her father-in-law and her husband were there, as was Mr. Wickham.

"Oh! I am sorry! I did not realize that you were busy. I will return another time." Elizabeth blushed and turned to go, her hand on the door ready to pull it shut.

"No, my dear, do not go. We are all but finished here," Papa George entreated. "I know that Fitzwilliam has been anxiously awaiting you." He teased his son, glancing at him with a smile.

Fitzwilliam blushed. Bowing to his father and nodding to Wickham, he quickly strode to his wife, taking her hand and placing it on his arm. Escorting her down the hall to a sitting room, he closed the door behind them and pulled Elizabeth into his arms, leaning down to give her a kiss.

"I have missed you today," he murmured, lips hovering over hers. "What have you been doing while I was stuck in the study all morning?" He tenderly kissed her again, then rested his head on hers, holding her close to his chest.

"Mmmm." Elizabeth moaned as she snuggled into his embrace. "I spent part of the morning with Mrs. Reynolds, finalizing menus for the family's visit. After that, I went for a walk."

"Lizzy …"

"I did not go outside, darling," she interrupted, knowing he was about to reiterate his admonishment for her to stay indoors. "I walked the hallways upstairs. I am sure the maids are not yet used to seeing me wandering around the place in that manner. I know at least one was startled to see me." Elizabeth giggled into his waistcoat and felt his chuckle begin in his chest before escaping his mouth in a deep, low roll.

"Ah, my love, I can imagine the looks you received." Fitzwilliam laughed, thinking of some unsuspecting maid coming out of a room and nearly being run over by his spouse.

"Is your meeting finished, husband?"

"Indeed it is. I am free to spend the remainder of the day by your side."

"Excellent!" Elizabeth smiled up at him, eyes sparkling, as she squeezed his middle. "Will you take me for a walk? And then perhaps sit with me in our sitting room before the fire and read with me before dinner? I have missed that so much recently." The two had made a habit since their marriage of spending time in a similar manner every afternoon and evening, but once the harvest had begun, Fitzwilliam had been out on the estate, supervising the gathering of the crops and directing their disbursement to storage areas, tenants, and mills. He came home just in time to eat, and was so weary that they frequently retired to their rooms after just a short time in the music room or library.

It was now December and the harvest was complete, as well as the myriad of winter-preparation tasks that were required. The wheat had been threshed and ground, the straw stacked, the produce stored, and the animals corralled near the barns. However, the work for Fitzwilliam and his father was not over. The time had come to plan for the next season, deciding what to plant and where. They examined the amounts reaped from the crops planted this year, and discussed the new farming methods they had read about and wanted to implement next spring. It was all rather interesting to Elizabeth, and she listened attentively whenever the subject came up in conversation. However, she longed to spend more time alone with her handsome husband, hence today's request.

Hearing her inquiry, Fitzwilliam was struck by a similar longing to spend more time with Elizabeth. He and his father had been working hard for the last couple of months. His father seemed to be more easily fatigued, and that concerned him, so he had taken on a far larger role this autumn than he had expected to.

"I would greatly enjoy spending the afternoon

with you in such a manner. Come, let us go inform Father where we will be and get our coats."

He offered his arm with a warm smile. Elizabeth tucked her hand in the crook of his elbow; her grin was brilliant. The two spent a splendid couple of hours wandering the grounds, until Elizabeth's red nose and slight shiver convinced Fitzwilliam that they had been out too long, and he insisted that they return indoors.

Once inside, the couple rested in the private sitting room of their suite of rooms in the family wing of the house for a while, before moving into the bedroom. After enjoying each other for a time, they lay cuddled together under the covers, chatting about the dinner they were planning to attend that evening. Once she heard Fitzwilliam's breathing even out, Elizabeth began contemplating the event and what might happen.

She was not nervous about the event, necessarily. She knew that her husband and Papa George would stand behind her and support her. They had proved that beyond the shadow of a doubt during the season when several of high society's matrons and their disappointed daughters and nieces had made her life miserable for a time. Despite the very obvious manner in which Lady Matlock had shown her off and displayed the family's support for all to see, there were families in town who had risked the censure of the House of Matlock to express their displeasure at her "capture" of one of their most sought-after bachelors. The ladies of these families had spread malicious speculation about her and her background and questioned her in a most severe manner at every ball, dinner, and visit she had attended.

Many were the nights she cried in Fitzwilliam's

arms on the way home from a soiree, and many were the angry visits he and his father made to the fathers and husbands of her tormenters. As time went on, with the reassurance of Fitzwilliam's love and Papa George's support, she began to regain her confidence. Her wit, displayed most frequently when she was angry or upset, began to reassert itself. Her smile became more genuine and less strained, and her laugh became more honest and sincere.

She was, however, forever changed. When amongst new acquaintances she was quiet and watchful. She lost much of the spontaneity that had characterized her before her marriage. She did not put herself forth to begin conversations until she had carefully watched the ladies and gentlemen and felt she had a good grasp of their character and if they were sincere. She was especially wary of the gentlemen. If she took the time to think about it, she began to be distressed at what Lord Regis had taken from her. But since she was not formed for unhappiness, she quickly pushed such thoughts away and focused on the good in her new life.

No, she was not what she would call nervous about tonight's dinner, but she did have some feelings of trepidation. She knew she would probably go through some of the same things she had in London during the season. She was not pleased to face such assaults again, but she supposed it was a fact of life. She reminded herself that Papa George and Fitzwilliam would take care of any person who dared insult her. Let them do their worst, she thought. It is nothing I have not faced before and ended the victor.

The Darcys were engaged for an event at a neighboring estate later that day. The current master, Mr.

John Miller, was good friends with Mr. Darcy. Fitzwilliam was a year or so older than the heir of Miller's Landing. He was the same age as the family's youngest daughter, Edith.

John Miller was of the belief that men of his society did not lower themselves to marry women who had relatives in trade. His shock upon learning that one of his oldest friends had brokered a marriage between his heir and such a woman had been great. Miller had never visited Pemberley when Elizabeth and her relatives were there, nor had he allowed his children to become friendly with them. He had railed long and loud to his family about the union before coming to the realization that, in the interest of maintaining an important connection, he had best modify his stance and at least behave in a manner that indicated his acceptance of it. Unfortunately, his attitude had seeped down to his only child still at home. Even more unfortunately, at least for her, his daughter was not inclined to accept the new mistress of Pemberley under any circumstances for any reason.

Edith Miller had once fancied herself the perfect Mrs. Darcy. In the same manner as many other young women of the first circles, she had kept her eye on Fitzwilliam Darcy over the years, eagerly awaiting his entrance into society's social whirl. Her shock upon hearing of his marriage so soon after his return from an abbreviated Grand Tour was immense. The identity of his new wife was equally astonishing. The niece of Mr. Darcy's friend in trade! Of course, Edith had never met the young lady. She was a gentleman's daughter, whose father opposed the friendship of his neighbor with a tradesman. Miss Miller could only suppose that the new Mrs. Darcy was brash and uneducated, and most certainly undeserving of the position she now enjoyed. Edith had every intention of letting the upstart know that she did not now nor ever would fit in with Derbyshire's elite.

Lady Susan Miller had initially shared her husband's feelings. She was, however, the first to realize that perhaps it would be best not to initiate a rift between two of the most prominent families in Derbyshire society. Indeed, she had heard some very good things from her friends in London about the young lady in question. While the Darcy and Miller families had not crossed paths during the Season, they had many acquaintances in common who had shared with her their impressions. It was Lady Susan who had persuaded her spouse to moderate his position, though she had less success convincing their daughter to do the same.

Upon their arrival at Miller's Landing, the Darcys were greeted enthusiastically by the master and mistress of the house. The eldest Millers were delighted with the beautiful though slightly reserved young woman. Regardless of their feelings toward their neighbor's friendship with a man in trade, the girl – for anyone could see that she was very young – was now married into the Darcy family and it behooved them to treat her with respect. It was not worth ruining a friendship of decades to be unaccepting of Fitzwilliam's wife.

"Mrs. Darcy!" exclaimed Lady Susan, holding Elizabeth's hands and smiling. "How delightful to finally meet you! We have heard such good things of you. What a shame we were unable to become acquainted before now!"

Elizabeth was a little uncomfortable with Lady Susan's enthusiasm. One of the changes resulting from her trials in the late winter and early spring of the year was that she had become more wary of strangers than had previously been her wont. However, she bravely put her best foot forward, secure in the knowledge that her husband and father-in-law were beside her. As a matter of fact, she could feel Fitzwilliam's hand resting on her back as she spoke.

"Lady Susan, it is an honor to meet you, as well. You have a beautiful home." Elizabeth smiled sweetly, relieved to feel her husband's thumb rubbing up and down the small of her back. He kept her anchored in such situations, and his prodigious care of her was greatly appreciated. After exchanging a few more pleasantries with their hostess and then her spouse, the young Darcy couple wandered into the drawing room where the rest of the guests were gathered. The pair made a circuit of the room, greeting those who had already met Elizabeth and making sure she was introduced to those few she was not previously acquainted with. Soon, their path led them to Edith Miller.

"Miss Miller," Darcy said, as he bowed to her, "may I present to you my wife, Elizabeth. Darling, this is Edith Miller. She is the middle of the Miller's three children. She, her siblings, and I were frequent visitors to each other's homes when we were all young. We shared many adventures."

"It is so nice to meet someone who can share tales of my husband's youth." Elizabeth smiled at the lady as she rose from her curtsey.

"Indeed," Miss Miller intoned, barely nodding in her guest's direction before turning to Fitzwilliam. "Mr. Fitzwilliam Darcy, how delightful it is to see you here!" Her tone with him was much more friendly and inviting than it had been with his wife, and Fitzwilliam was not happy. No one treated Elizabeth ill and got away with it.

"Indeed," he replied, in a tone similar to hers with his spouse, barely nodding before moving Elizabeth along to greet someone else. Outwardly, he was calm and stern-looking as ever, but inside he was seething. What is she about? he wondered. Surely she knows that it is not to her benefit to be unwelcoming to a Darcy! His tension was quickly noted by his very perceptive wife, and she surreptitiously squeezed the arm she was holding. Glancing down at her and seeing her twinkling eyes gazing at him, he relaxed a bit. She truly was a glorious woman, and he was beyond blessed to have her. Thank you, Papa, for arranging this marriage. I will be forever grateful, he thought.

Miss Miller watched the couple walk away. She was angry that Fitzwilliam had treated her as he had, and she was even angrier that he was smiling at that woman. True, the marriage was made and there was nothing she could do about it. That did not, however, mean that the little baggage should or would be accepted by society. Edith determined that she was going to do what she could tonight to start Mrs. Darcy's downfall.

She began by criticizing Elizabeth's dress and manner to the gentleman sitting to her left. She quietly made accusation in the ears of the one on her right that the young lady was flirting with every man in the room. To the young lady across the table, Miss Miller spoke of Mrs. Darcy's rumored lack of dowry.

Before long, her parents caught on to what she was doing and her mother spoke to her, urging, almost demanding, that she stop. But Miss Miller failed to recognize that her parents were against her and that the rest of society would be as well, and she ignored their censuring words. Soon she would learn the dire consequences of spreading gossip and lies about her neighbor.

All through dinner, as Edith worked her neighbors and friends, the Darcys chatted and smiled and laughed, clearly enjoying the food and the company. The sight of Mr. Darcy enjoying himself was rare enough. He did not get out as much now that his wife was departed this world, and he had a tendency toward sadness that was palpable. It was the sight of young Fitzwilliam behaving in a lively manner that shocked the guests, most of whom had known him his entire life. Even when his dear mother had been alive, he had been quiet and reserved, and this tendency had grown after her death. Many could not account for it, but others recognized that his newfound joy probably came from his delight with his young wife.

After dinner, the ladies retired to the drawing room to enjoy a cup of tea and some time to visit. Being the social creature she was, Elizabeth was not unduly concerned about conversing with virtual strangers. What was disquieting were the looks she had noticed she was receiving during the meal from those sitting on either side of her host's daughter. They had ranged from pity to outright disgust. She was unsure what she would be facing here, but as always, her courage rose with every attempt to intimidate her. She was a gentleman's daughter and the daughter-in-law of a very powerful man. She knew that she had the support of her spouse and his family. Her chin rose as Edith Miller and another guest approached.

"Mrs. Darcy, such a pleasure to have you join us."

"Thank you, Miss Miller. I have heard so much about you from my Fitzwilliam and his father," Elizabeth replied with a smile.

"Indeed. I understand you are from Hertford-shire?"

"Yes, my father's estate is called Longbourn."

"Your father has an estate? What a surprise! I did not think that a tradesman would have a landowner in his family. And the name of the estate is Longbourn, you say? I do not think I have ever heard of it. It must be quite small and insignificant."

"I am not surprised that you have never heard of it; it really is of little importance except to those who live there. As for the other, there are a good many tradesmen who have gentlemen in their family. It is not all that uncommon for a younger son to take up a trade. One must earn a living when one is not the heir. Indeed, gentlemen in need of funds to save the family estate are now looking to the daughters of tradesmen for wives. Many have quite attractive dowries." Elizabeth laughed to herself. Really, Miss Miller was quite obvious.

Ignoring most of her opponent's statement, Edith continued her attack. "I am surprised, then, that you ever met the Darcy family. Surely a family as exalted as they would not bother with an insignificant estate in such an unimportant county." Her sneer was subtle, but obvious to Elizabeth, who had remained alert so as to determine the form of attack her adversary would use. Now that she knew the direction the conversation was taking, she let her charm and artless manner take over.

"I was certain you knew that my father-in-law and my uncle are great friends, and that my sister and I spent a month each summer at Pemberley for oh, a couple of years at least. I do not see how it would be the least surprising that Fitzwilliam and I would make a match."

By this time, several more of Edith's friends had joined the group, some eager to watch her cut down the newcomer to their circle and others uneasy about bringing pain to a member of the most important family in the area.

Elizabeth continued. "My father Darcy and my uncle were certainly aware of the attraction, even if Pemberley's neighbors were not." Elizabeth smiled at her interrogator. She had often been able to deflect censure for sharp words with her engaging smile.

Miss Miller's lips pinched and her eyes narrowed. Her face froze in an expression of anger and insult. It seemed that she recognized the rebuke in Elizabeth's words for what they were. Her friends fell silent as they waited to see what Edith would do.

"Indeed." Miss Miller turned and walked stiffly away with a disdainful smile on her face and her faithful followers in her wake. Her target breathed a sigh of relief; the first battle of the night had been fought, and she had come out the victor. She hoped the rest of the evening went as well.

Unfortunately for Elizabeth, the war was not over. No sooner had the crowd cleared from around her than another lady walked up to her and began a conversation. This lady, an aunt to one of the young ladies who had been clustered about her earlier, wasted no time voicing mindless pleasantries, instead commencing her conversation with a barely concealed insult.

"My husband and I were rather surprised to see Mr. Darcy so willing to form an alliance between his heir and the relation of a tradesman."

Elizabeth sighed to herself, then smiled sweetly at her companion. "Indeed. You are not the only one to feel that way, I believe. And yet, he did. It must not have been such a surprise to him."

The lady was shocked at Elizabeth's impertinence. Her mouth hung open for a heartbeat or so before she snapped it shut and moved on.

And so it continued for the next thirty minutes or so. Elizabeth moved about the room, being as sociable as possible under the conditions. She was careful to examine each person's countenance and attitude, trying to determine who was genuinely interested in becoming a friend and who was simply out for information or to break her down. She was distressed by many of the comments of her detractors. Insinuations were made that she was too coarse because she smiled, that her husband had watched her so closely at dinner because he was looking to make sure she did not embarrass the family, and that she was not good enough to be Mrs. Darcy. Apparently, no one had noticed that she gazed at Fitzwilliam just as often as he did her. It seemed that none of them knew what it was to love their husband so deeply that to be at the other end of the table was distressing.

Elizabeth battled as best she could, projecting a calm demeanor in the face of the negativity, using her wit when required to fend off attacks, and engaging with appreciation those who appeared to genuinely desire her company. Encounters of such a sort were tiring, though, and when Fitzwilliam entered the room with the rest of the gentlemen, he immediately ascertained the distress in her eyes. He strode quickly over to her, glancing at the woman speaking to her, whose back was to him. As he reached the pair, he overheard some of what his Elizabeth had been going through.

The lady was Edith Miller, come back for another go at discomposing his wife.

"I am sure, Mrs. Darcy, that your husband Fitzwilliam is quite cognizant of his place in society. He keeps a close eye on you, I noticed. He must be quite concerned that you understand it, as well."

Fitzwilliam was angry. Enraged, even. He stepped up next to his wife and took her hand, tucking it in his elbow and pulling it in tight to his side. "Indeed not, madam. My wife is a well-bred woman. I can trust her perfectly well with the

Darcy family's reputation. She would never think of doing anything that would degrade our name or embarrass herself or her family. It is a shame that not every gentlewoman is as worthy of the title as my Elizabeth is. Excuse me, Father, Mr. Miller; I need to speak to my wife in private."

With a last glare at his host's daughter, Fitzwilliam stiffly but gently led Elizabeth out of the room and into the hall. Once there, he looked around for a quiet place to take her. He settled upon the library, which he knew from previous visits was two doors further down. Once there, he shut the door behind him and turned, pulling his wife into his arms.

"Are you well, my darling?" He whispered into her hair as he held her tightly to him. He tried to keep the anger out of his voice. She was upset enough. There was no need to further alarm her with a harsh voice or irate words.

Elizabeth snuggled into his chest and sighed. This was her favorite place to be, held close to her partner and wrapped in his arms. That they were in a library, with the smell of leather bindings and paper, just added to the feeling of safety.

"I am now, dearest," she replied.

"You are certain? I could see by the look in your eyes that Miss Miller had distressed you. Was it only she doing so? Surely my brave and coura-geous wife would not be made so after one per-son made a comment to her. How long did it go on, Elizabeth? Who joined her?" Now that he had her in his arms, Fitzwilliam began to relax. Being with her always made him so, though he was still very angry.

"I am certain. I was upset for a while, but now that I am alone with you, I am comforted. I was very much glad to see you enter the room. I am not sure how much longer I could have held out and still called myself a lady." She hugged his waist a little tighter. Surely she was the most blessed woman in the world to have such a husband. She trusted him implicitly, for he always had her best interests at heart and always stood up for her.

"I am happy to have prevented such an occurrence. You avoided one of my questions, though, Mrs. Darcy. Were more ladies than Miss Miller rude to you?"

Elizabeth sighed, then leaned back a bit so she could look into his face. "Indeed, Fitzwilliam. The only ladies who were not so were Lady Susan, Mrs. Burns, Mrs. Morris, and the Shetler ladies. Those five were exceedingly kind."

"My father and I will take care of this, Elizabeth.

You have my assurance."

"Thank you, husband. I knew you would. May we stay here a little while longer? I have need of more comfort." She spoke with a grin and a raised eyebrow.

Fitzwilliam chuckled. "I believe that is possible," he said as he bent his head down to kiss her.

It was quite a while later that the couple finally returned to the party, holding hands, with flushed faces, slightly disheveled looks, and happy smiles.

~~~***~~~

Edith Miller had not seen the men trickling in from the dining room. She was startled, therefore, at the male voice behind her, and had the grace to look ashamed at being caught berating Mrs. Darcy by her husband. She was also quite fearful, as to her left and next to the obviously
~~~

offended Fitzwilliam Darcy appeared her father and the elder Darcy. Her father had warned her earlier to cease and desist her disparagement of their neighbor's son's wife, but she had ignored him. There would be consequences now that she would have to face. While her father had never been mean, she knew he would be quite harsh with her. She hated Mrs. Darcy but feared her father's disapprobation more.

"Edith, you are to retire to your chambers immediately. We will discuss this later." Mr. Miller gave her a look that brooked no disobedience; therefore, Miss Miller immediately left the room without taking leave of her mother and the guests. Everyone had stopped what they were doing to watch, and so they all knew that she had been summarily dismissed and none were offended at her lack of manners. Her accomplices were shocked that she was banished in such a manner.

Miller looked to his friend. "Darcy, I apologize. I told Edith earlier to discontinue her disdain of your daughter-in-law. Obviously, she ignored me. I will speak to her again."

"I appreciate your efforts. However, I must tell you, and everyone here, that if Elizabeth is not accepted among you, then neither are Georgiana, Fitzwilliam or I. She is a Darcy, the same as the rest of us. I will not tolerate mistreatment of any of my children, including Fitzwilliam's wife." Darcy's displeasure was clear to all, and he spoke in firm, ringing tones. He was intent on making his point clear to everyone in the room. He knew that word of this incident would spread. While he did not like his family to be the target of gossip, he was not about to let his dear daughter-in-law suffer due to the rude and arrogant behavior of his neighbors.

After making this statement and being assured of the understanding of the other guests of his meaning, he glanced around at the interested gazes of his companions and suggested to his host that they retire to the study, or somewhere else more private. Gesturing toward the door, Mr. Miller agreed and the two men made their way to the study.

After pouring his guest a glass of port and inviting him to sit, Miller braced himself for what was to come. He could only hope that his nearest neighbor and the most influential man in this half of Derbyshire would not sever the acquaintance between their families. They were old friends, it was true, but Darcys were known for their family loyalty. Neither George Darcy nor his son was going to take this lying down, he knew. There would be repercussions of some sort or other.

Darcy took a sip of his port as he gathered his thoughts together. Finally, he spoke. "We have been neighbors and friends all our lives. I cannot describe to you the depth of my disappointment that it was your daughter, of all people, who hurt my daughter in such a way." His countenance clearly showed his unhappiness and displeasure.

"I cannot let this pass, my friend, you know this. There must be some consequence for Miss Miller. And, should she behave similarly to Elizabeth in the future, I would be left with no choice but to sever our friendship."

Miller replied, "I understand, Darcy. I will take immediate action with Edith. Her aunt in Sussex has been asking her to visit. I believe I will send her tomorrow for an extended stay. Again I beg your pardon. I do not know what has gotten into her."

Darcy nodded his acceptance of the apology.

"That sounds like a reasonable solution. I trust you will impress upon your daughter the importance of regulating her conduct."

Miller took note that this was a statement, not a question. He thought to himself, Oh, you can be quite certain of that, old friend! Aloud he simply stated, "I will," glad that he still had Darcy's good opinion.

The two gentlemen soon finished their port and returned to the drawing room.

Early the next morning, while their guests still slept, Edith Miller and her maid entered one of the family's travelling coaches for an extended visit to her mother's sister. Her father had been every bit as severe as she had expected. He had explained to her in explicit detail what would happen to her should he lose the approbation of one of his oldest friends, who just happened to be the most powerful man in Derbyshire. While she was angry at her banishment, and confused at her father's apparent change of heart regarding Mrs. Darcy, she was astute enough to realize that being the cause of a break between the two families would hurt the standing of the Millers and therefore her chances to make a good match. To Sussex she would go, quietly, and contemplate her choices.

Chapter 12

Upon their return to Pemberley the next morning, the family was delighted to find the mail had made it through the wintry weather. In addition to letters of business for George and Fitzwilliam Darcy was an eagerly-anticipated letter for Elizabeth from her elder sister and dearest friend, Jane.

The two young women had always been close, sharing confidences as well as a bed. Jane was opposite Elizabeth in almost every way. She was tall and willowy where her sister was shorter, petite, but with a womanly form. She was very reserved in company, always wearing a serene smile no matter what was going on around her, and she always saw the best in everyone. Elizabeth, on the other hand, had always been gregarious, enjoyed social events, and was quick to form judgements of people. She still did enjoy social situations; she was simply more cautious in them than in previous years and now took longer to analyse characters. Both girls were very intelligent. Many times, new acquaintances took Jane's serenity and desire to see only good as a sign that she lacked cleverness. Those who knew her well were quite aware that Jane perceived more of what was going on around her than she let on, and when she felt she was right, she could be quite immovable.

Thanking her father-in-law for the letter, Elizabeth excused herself and made her way quickly to her private study. Entering the room, a smile lit her face at the grace and elegance expressed by the decoration. She had made no changes to this chamber upon her marriage, and it was exactly as her predecessor, Lady Anne Darcy, had left it. Elizabeth loved the room as it was. Lady Anne had been a talented decorator, turning Pemberley into a gorgeous yet understated home. Elizabeth had become familiar with the duties of mistress, and was more comfortable with that role after several months of marriage. Yet, for all that she was married to the heir and her husband and father insisted she consider herself the mistress, Elizabeth still had moments when she felt uncomfortable with it. She did not want to take Lady Anne's place. So, she had learned all that was required of the position, but left everything as the true holder of that title had arranged it.

Sitting down upon the settee near the fireplace, Elizabeth opened her letter, smiling at the descriptions of life at Longbourn.

My Dearest Lizzy,

How are you, my dearest sister, and your husband and family? Are you well? Your descriptions of a decorated Pemberley continue to thrill us all. What an amazing number of rooms you have kept open for the holiday! And all the servants … how do you keep them all straight, for I know you, Lizzy, and I know that you have taken the trouble to learn the names of each. What a caring mistress they have gained!

How are you to celebrate the Christmas season there in Derbyshire? You must write soon with all the details!

Please do not be angry with me, dear sister, when you hear that I have kept from you things that I was afraid would worry you. You have had so much happening in your new life that I did not want to add to your burden. Indeed, these things are not so very bad at all, but recent events have caused them to escalate, and I no longer feel that I can keep them from you.

Here at Longbourn, we are to celebrate in the usual manner, with Aunt and Uncle Gardiner and the children. They arrived yesterday just in time for tea. How the little ones have grown! Papa and Uncle soon took themselves to the library, and Aunt sent the children up to the nursery with our younger sisters before she began taking Mama to task for her part in the confrontation the two of you had in the summer when you visited, about your marriage to Fitzwilliam. I was surprised to be allowed to stay in the room, but Aunt declared that since I have been paying a price for defending you, I should hear what she had to say. I have not mentioned this before, but Mama has been very upset with me for the last several months. While I know that I deserve her censure for speaking so to her, I do not regret it. I was right to defend you, and I would do it again were it required of me. However, I now have a much greater understanding of your propensity to take walks! But I digress.

As I said, Aunt Gardiner began to take Mama to task and at first, Mama could not think of anything to say, not that Aunt gave her opportunity to speak. When Mama did gather herself and began, my Aunt simply held her hand up and stated that she would listen and when it was her turn to speak Aunt would let her know. I was shocked when Mama snapped her mouth closed immediately, but I could see the anger on her face. I will admit I was anxious. I am sure it showed in my face as well, for Aunt soon reached over to me and grasped my hand before turning her conversation to Mama's treatment of me. When she was finally given leave to speak, Mama loudly proclaimed her innocence and tried to blame both you and me for what happened.

Oh, Lizzy! How can she not see her part in it? Is she truly so blind to her actions? She must be. She must be unable to see beyond herself and to how she affects others. We must be forgiving, Lizzy, and I know you will be. Indeed, I know you have already forgiven her. Your heart is so tender that it cannot be otherwise!

As for Papa, you can, I am sure, imagine his response to the upheaval all these months. He remained in his book room much of the time, per his usual habit. He offered me some respite there a few times and gave me some advice. He said that if I were patient, Mama would blow herself out sooner or later and turn her agitation elsewhere. I know he was sincere, but I will risk sounding ungrateful by saying that I was not comforted by it, and I have many times wished he would exert himself to calm her.

In any case, my mother has regulated her behavior towards me. I cannot but wait and see if it continues after Aunt and Uncle leave. I know from Aunt that Papa and Uncle had a similar discussion, though it was less heated than the one in the drawing room. They feel that Papa should have made a better effort, after all that has happened, to shield you from Mama. They are aware that Mr. Darcy and your husband do not wish to allow you to visit us again, as they do not trust Mama. I agree with them—it is unfair for your sisters to lose your company because my parents do not behave as they ought.

Mary continues with her pianoforte lessons, and she practices almost constantly between them. She has found a book of Fordyce's sermons somewhere, probably from Papa's library. She has devoured it and has begun adding quotes from it to her regular recital of Scriptures.

Lydia and Kitty continue as they always have. They are doing well in their lessons, though they are eager to quit them every day. They are much happier learning needlework and how to trim bonnets than they are reading and doing sums. I am afraid, dear sister, that they may never learn to appreciate the written word as you and Papa have. Even I, who prefers novels to Shakespeare, like reading better than our youngest sisters. Not everyone is the same, however, and I am sure they will do well in life regardless.

I know you have impatiently read this letter through, wanting me to get to what you would term "the most important part," and I shall make you wait no longer. You know, of course, that Mr. Bingley and I spent much of your ball speaking to each other, and that I was quite intrigued by him. You also know he called on me several times at my aunt and uncle's in the weeks following. He has since made regular trips to Longbourn to visit. Mama has, as you would expect, made a great deal of fuss over it, insisting he stay here overnight. I confess to staring in awe at her a few times, for even as she pressed him to stay and pushed him at me, she berated me for my disrespect. But I digress. You will be happy to know that Mr. Bingley has asked me for a courtship, and I have consented. Papa declared he was delighted to give his consent, and the rest of my family expressed equal felicitations. Perhaps with this, Mama will finally forgive me fully.

Give my love to your Darcy family, and accept

ours from here. We miss your presence but are grateful for your safety and happiness.

Your sister,

Jane Bennet

Elizabeth was not surprised at the revelation that her London relatives had chastised her family. It was to them that her father had sent her after Lord Regis had assaulted her. It was they who had arranged her marriage to her beloved Fitzwilliam. They loved her and defended her as their own child. Elizabeth loved her parents, but it was the Gardiners to whom she had learned to turn in times of need.

Fitzwilliam found his wife there, in her study, staring into space with her letter in her hand. "Sweetheart?" He was surprised to see her so contemplative.

At the sound of his voice, she jumped. "Oh, I did not hear you come in! I am sorry!" She smiled at him and grasped the hand he held out to her as he lowered himself beside her on the settee. She rearranged her position so that she could cuddle up into his side with her feet tucked up under her skirts.

"Was there bad news from Longbourn?" Fitzwilliam wrapped his arms around his sweet wife and held her tightly to his side. She had suffered much in the last year from her mother's antics, and he dearly hoped the woman was not up to her old tricks again.

"No, not really. It seems Aunt Gardiner had something to say to Mama about our battle in the summer." She handed the letter to him. "Here, it will be easier if you read it yourself."

He took the letter with some trepidation; he was

in a very good mood and was not sure he wanted that disturbed. However, the further into the missive he got, the more he relaxed. Jane had included no details about her mother's response, though he knew enough of the woman to be able to imagine what was said.

"I am delighted to see that though Jane maintains her ability to reason away the behavior of others, she does see the impropriety of it all. Do you think it will make a difference?"

"I do not know. It is hard to say. Jane says she is behaving well with the Gardiners there, but Mama may just be biding her time so she can explode when they are gone. Jane may need to go to London to stay for a while with my aunt and uncle come February or March."

"We will be going in late January. Why do we not invite her to visit? We can take her to the theater and some balls and entertain her well. We will have to attend these events anyway; why not take Jane with us?"

"Really, Fitzwilliam? That would be wonderful! Papa George will approve, will he not?" Elizabeth's face glowed with her excitement, making her husband smile broadly.

"Oh yes; you know that Father loves Jane almost as much as he loves you. He has told me that he is doubly glad, after meeting your mother and seeing the home you grew up in, that you had such a close sister to cling to all those years. He thinks very highly of her."

"How wonderful! Thank you, darling! I will write to her now and invite her." With that, Elizabeth popped up off the settee and over to her desk to write to her most beloved sister.

The next day, the Darcy family was surprised by

visits from some of their neighbors. The first to visit was the Millers. Elizabeth, Fitzwilliam, and Mr. Darcy settled into the yellow drawing room with their guests, calling for tea and refreshments. The Millers had come with a purpose and quickly got to the point.

Lady Susan was sitting in a chair near Elizabeth's, and turned to her after greetings were given to say, "My dear Mrs. Darcy, I feel that I must apologize again for Edith's unkindness towards you. I did try to steer her away from such actions, and I feel that I have failed as a parent because she ignored me. My eyes have been opened to what my behavior has been that led to her belief that her words and deeds would be acceptable."

She looked down to her lap, a frown on her face. When she brought her gaze up again, she reached over and took Elizabeth's hand and with an earnest expression, continued. "I know that you have no other women living close to you, and I would like to offer my friendship to you. I am aware that I and my family have really given you little cause to trust us, but my offer is sincere. I have much for which to atone. I like you, and I am amazed at the changes you have brought to the Darcy men. Please, Mrs. Darcy, say that you forgive me. Allow me to make it up to you in this way."

Elizabeth had kept her eyes focused on Lady Susan's face during this speech and believed that she saw sincerity. She remembered that at the Millers' dinner, this was one of the ladies present who had been nice to her, and made her feel welcome. She did wonder for a moment if the lady was only saying these things to maintain a friendship with the Darcy family. However, she was determined not to be cynical. She looked up at Papa George, who gave her a small, encouraging smile and a nod, then to her husband, whose hand was resting on her shoulder. He gave her a nod and a squeeze, and she knew that both the men in her life had spoken to Mr. Miller and felt the offer was genuine, and that it was up to her to decide.

Looking back at Lady Susan, Elizabeth made her decision. She had faith that this was an honest proposal. "Thank you, madam. I appreciate your honesty, and your willingness to change. I do forgive you, and I accept your offer of friendship." Elizabeth smiled and squeezed the hand that held hers as the men in the room breathed a sigh of relief and sent a silent prayer of thanks heavenward.

The Millers stayed another fifteen minutes or so

before leaving to make a stop in Lambton and then go home. They had not been gone thirty minutes when Mrs. Reynolds announced another visitor.

"Mrs. Robert Shetler and Miss Shetler." Mrs. Reynolds curtsied and left the room, shutting the doors behind her.

Mr. Darcy greeted the newcomers first, bowing and asking after them. Fitzwilliam and Elizabeth followed suit and when the greetings were completed, everyone settled into their seats. They made small talk while a maid brought in a fresh tea tray, and Elizabeth poured out. The Darcy men had no intention of leaving Elizabeth alone with two women whose opinions about and attitudes toward her were unknown. If this made the women uneasy, they did not let on.

The Shetler ladies were the wife and daughter of

a local landowner and gentleman farmer. They had been in attendance at the Millers' dinner and witnessed Miss Miller's treatment of the young Mrs. Darcy. The pair were friendly and loving women and had been appalled at the things that had been said and done. They had discussed it that evening after the party and with Mr. Shetler's blessing were here to offer their friendship to a young woman, as they saw it, in need. They were not as high as the Darcys, but if they read the family correctly, that would not matter.

"Mrs. Darcy," began Mrs. Shetler, "I wanted to come to you today and apologize for the way you were treated at the Millers' dinner. I was shocked that Edith could act in such a way. I have never seen anything like that from her before."

"Thank you," Elizabeth replied. "I do not know

Miss Miller well enough to know how she acts out of my presence, but it is a comfort to know that it was out of the ordinary. To be sure, I had similar experiences in London following my marriage, so I was not shocked. It is, however, nice to know that there are those who do not approve of such behavior."

Elizabeth remembered thinking at the dinner that she really liked the Shetler women. They appeared very genuine, with no airs or behaviors that would suggest otherwise. As Miss Shetler added her comments to the conversation, Elizabeth began to realize that this young woman, close in age to herself, had the makings for a friend. As always, she was watchful, and she looked frequently to her husband and father to see what indications they were giving her. Seeing nothing in their expressions or actions that indicated she should not, Elizabeth did something she had not done in almost a year—she invited her neighbor to visit again soon.

"Oh, I would be delighted! Thank you! I confess I had hoped that we could be friends, but I had not anticipated an invitation so soon." Miss Shetler's happiness and pleasure shone in her eyes and wide smile. "Thank you again! There are so few gentlewomen our age in the area that it is a joy to meet a new one!" She blushed at that statement, and Elizabeth laughed.

"Indeed, I believe you are correct. Thank you for consenting. I am anticipating becoming good friends."

The Shetler ladies stayed a few minutes longer before they, too, made their way elsewhere. When they were gone, the Darcy men expressed their happiness to Elizabeth at her impulsiveness. They had feared that she would never feel confident enough again to invite someone to be

close to her without their explicit approval. She in

turn expressed her surprise at herself and thank-

fulness that she would have a friend.

Chapter 13

A few more days passed, and soon the Darcy family was expecting a large number of house-guests for the holiday week. Charles Bingley, Fitzwilliam's best school chum, was to arrive first, along with his sister Caroline. Soon after, the Earl and Countess of Matlock, along with their sons, Lieutenant Richard Fitzwilliam and Viscount Tansley and his wife, the Viscountess Tansley, were to arrive. Also close to the Darcys and important to the family were the Morris and Burns families. Closing out the list of guests was the Millers, John and Lady Susan. There would be a few families, such as the Shetlers, who would attend various dinners as well as the ball, who would not be staying as part of the house party.

The Burns family was the complete opposite of the Millers. This family consisted of husband Scott, wife Agatha, and two children and their spouses, Abner and Rebecca Burns and George and Elspeth O' Grady. The Burns patriarch was a happy-go-lucky sort of man; his wife was equally jolly. They had raised their children to be the same. Every member of the family expressed their sincere delight at the marriage upon seeing Mrs. Darcy. They had met the lady previously and had known her to be delightful. In their collective opinion, anyone who had observed Fitzwilliam and Elizabeth together in previous years would be able to see their attachment and would not be surprised at the union. The Burnses were delighted that the pair was so happy.

The Morris family was the next to arrive. Like John Miller and Scott Burns, Edward Morris was an old friend of George Darcy, and his sons had grown up with Fitzwilliam. Currently, his heir, Robert, was visiting his wife's family for the holidays; middle son Joshua was serving with His Majesty's forces and was unable to get leave until after the New Year; while youngest son Michael, a divinity student, was spending his holiday at the home of a friend.

Edward Morris was of two minds on the marriage his friend Darcy had arranged for his heir. Granted, the young lady in question was delightful. She was sure to bring a smile to anyone with whom she spoke. However, her uncle was in trade. He had struggled with what he should or should not say or do on the matter, until his wife pointed out that it was pointless to be concerned. The marriage was made and the only option open to them was to accept or reject it. Like the Millers, Mr. Morris and his good wife made the decision to accept and welcome the newest Darcy. Their battle had been blessedly shorter than that of the Millers.

Most eagerly anticipated by Elizabeth was Charles Bingley, whom she had met at her presentation ball in the spring, and who was now courting her sister Jane. Bingley and Fitzwilliam had met at Eton where they were in the same year, were the same age, and shared a room. Complete opposites in personality, they had quickly found themselves forming a strong and lasting bond of friendship. Fitzwilliam had defended Bingley against those who disparaged him for being the son of a tradesman, and Bingley defended Fitzwilliam against those who ridiculed him for his reserve and obvious homesickness. Their friendship had strengthened over time, as they helped each other through troubles and celebrated accomplishments together. Bingley brought levity and cheer to his friend, and Fitzwilliam assisted Bingley in navigating the social mores and customs of the higher society his merchant father expected him to enter.

Accompanying Bingley was his twin sister, Caroline. Fitzwilliam had met her on three or four previous occasions and had been less than impressed. She invariably attached herself to his arm, clinging like a limpet, her intent as clear as a sunny day. He could only hope that his marriage to Elizabeth had turned Miss Bingley's mind away from him and toward someone else … anyone else … who might actually appreciate her and envision making a life with her. Heaven only knew what his wife would do if his friend's sister behaved as she usually did in his presence! While Elizabeth was not sure enough of herself at this point to respond aggressively to attacks on her person, he knew from previous experience that she was passionate to defend those she loved.

Upon the Bingleys' arrival at Pemberley, it was obvious that Miss Caroline Bingley had not turned her attention away from Fitzwilliam. She did, however, have enough sense to know to treat Elizabeth well, at least in the presence of the lady's husband. He may no longer be in the market for a wife, but he was still the most handsome man she had ever met, and he was the heir to a large fortune. She would do well to remain in his good graces, even if it meant she had to be pleasant to the unknown interloper who had stolen him away.

She surprised no one in attendance who was already acquainted with her, when she immediately grabbed hold of Fitzwilliam's arm and held on tightly, while at the same time greeting his wife as enthusiastically as she was able, which was meagerly at best.

Fitzwilliam, knowing Elizabeth as well as he did, braced himself. A riveting confrontation was about to take place. He glanced at his wife with a look of trepidation. Deep down, though, he admitted to himself that he was looking forward to watching her put Miss Bingley in her place. He did not want her to make a scene, and was reasonably certain she would not, but he could see by her look that she was going to say something. He only hoped he did not visibly celebrate when she did. He missed this part of his wife's personality, and he was confident he would see it more often in future encounters, especially when she herself was the victim.

Elizabeth's eyebrows were lifted, and there was a definite spark of anger in her eyes as she took in Miss Bingley's grip on her husband. "Miss Bingley. How nice to finally meet you. I have heard so much about you from my darling husband." At this, she gave her adversary such a ferocious look that the woman paled. "Perhaps you are unaware of the etiquette required when a single woman and a married man greet. You are to allow him to bow over your hand, but you are not to touch him beyond that. It would be far too forward for a gently-bred lady to do otherwise."

Fitzwilliam bit back a smile. This was getting to be very interesting.

Caroline let go. Under no circumstances did she want to be seen as anything other than a gentlewoman. She endeavored to forget her roots in trade and did not want attention drawn to that uncomfortable fact. Too, Mrs. Darcy seemed rather fierce. One did not know of what a country miss such as she was capable. Perhaps, she thought, she ought to leave her effusions to a time when the other lady was not in the same room. Still, she seethed. Did not this country bumpkin know that she and Fitzwilliam were friends of long standing? Well, perhaps "friends" was too strong a word, but he was friends with her brother! Surely that counted!

"Indeed, Mrs. Darcy, I am aware of proper decorum. In my haste to greet my old friend, I forgot myself. I apologize." Her teeth were gritted; oh, how she would like to tear this woman to pieces with her words. Only the strongest of desires to be invited to this great estate in the future kept her in check.

"I am happy to hear it, Miss Bingley. Let us hope you are able to act with more restraint in the future." Elizabeth smiled sweetly, but her rival could see the warning – touch him again at your own peril!

"Come Miss Bingley, Mr. Bingley … Mrs. Reynolds will show you to your rooms. We have had to house you in the guest wing for this visit, as the earl and countess and their family have quite taken over the family wing." Waving her visitors toward the grand staircase, Elizabeth felt pleased with herself. She would be wary with this one, but knew that she would come out on top. After all, Fitzwilliam was hers, for the rest of their lives.

~~~***~~~

When the Matlocks arrived, there was much slapping of backs and kissing of hands. The family had not been together in this manner since the end of the season, and they were anticipating this time spent in each other's presence.

Part of the Matlock group was a young man of five and twenty years who was a friend of the viscount. The gentleman, Lord Perry Walton,
~~~

Baron Rockford, was just coming out of mourning for his father. An only son, he inherited everything the previous baron had owned, including a large amount of debt. Upon hearing from his cousin that Bingley's sister was to join the party, Lord Tansley had written Fitzwilliam, asking that Walton be invited. Fitzwilliam was more than happy to promote anything that would finally get Caroline Bingley married and out of his hair, so he gladly extended the invitation.

Lord Walton had been reluctant at first to impose upon a family with whom he was only loosely acquainted, but upon hearing that Miss Bingley's fortune was twenty thousand pounds, decided to make the trip. He had high hopes that she would meet his other requirements for a wife and that she would accept at least a courtship. Though to be honest, even if she looked like a horse and behaved like a donkey, with her dowry, she would be acceptable. He needed an infusion of cash, sooner rather than later!

The addition of another single gentleman was a relief to Lieutenant Fitzwilliam. He was aware of Caroline Bingley's pursuit of his cousin and had half-feared she would look to himself as an alternative. That Lord Walton was a first son made him far more eligible than a lowly second son in the army. The lieutenant determined to do everything he could to promote a match between the two.

Dinner this first night was not overly formal, beyond entering the dining room according to precedence. Guests were free to choose where they would sit, and Fitzwilliam insisted his wife sit next to him, as she usually did. He was at one end of the table and his father was at the other.

Miss Bingley was scandalized at this complete lack of proper etiquette, but gathered from her hosts that the decision to do away with proper seating arrangements for this night was made in deference to herself and the other guests, who were fatigued from travel. Rather than force everyone to behave with strict propriety, the Darcys were happy to let them all relax and enjoy themselves. She could not fathom doing such a thing at a party she hosted, but then she heard Mr. Darcy say that it was informal because it was a family dinner. She preened silently at the distinction of being considered so, and decided that it was perfectly acceptable to hold a dinner in such a manner for family.

Such was her focus on Mrs. Darcy and her perception of her hostess's lack of social graces that she failed to notice the titled gentleman who was the only eligible single man, other than her brother, in the party.

After dinner, the theme of informality was contin-ued. Rather than the men and women separating for a time, they all repaired to the music room. Elizabeth and the other young ladies, except for Georgiana, who could not be prevailed upon to do so, exhibited on the pianoforte and harp to the delight of everyone. Soon, all the guests gave in to their fatigue and retired for the night, followed by the Darcys.

For the first two or three days, the house party went rather well, at least to the casual observer. Elizabeth did not have cause to be alone in Miss Bingley's company, which was a relief. She did hear one or two remarks about her person and her manner come from the lady's lips that could be construed as snide or disparaging, but nothing that distressed her overly much. She had heard worse just last week at the Miller's dinner party.

The group kept busy during this time, with a tour of the house or a ride in the mornings, and billiards for the gentlemen and time in the parlor with needlework for the ladies in the afternoons. Evenings were spent in playing cards, or reading aloud, or even acting out short segments of favored works. Dinners were generally formal, complete with a division of the sexes immediately following the meal. This was the time of day Elizabeth dreaded most. Not because she was frightened or worried, but because she could see with each passing day that Caroline was finding it more and more difficult to rein in her tongue, and it was wearying to be constantly in battle.

Some of the matrons of the party, Lady Susan, Mrs. Burns, and Mrs. Morris, all noticed Miss Bingley's manner towards Elizabeth. They, knowing what had happened with Edith Miller, thought that perhaps this new young lady in their midst would benefit from a warning. They quietly decided amongst themselves to do so, and invited the countess and viscountess, who they knew to be supportive of their hostess, to join them. While Elizabeth was occupied with the other ladies, these five approached Caroline after dinner on the third full day of the party.

As the lady whose family had so far been the most affected by a negative reaction towards Elizabeth, and given that she had offered friendship to the young wife of her neighbor, Lady Susan was the first to speak. "Miss Bingley, I ... we ... have noticed your words and actions against Mrs. Darcy and feel that it would be in your best interest to warn you of the most likely consequences." She paused, looking around at her peers before giving her full attention once more to the younger woman.

Caroline opened her mouth to speak, but was cut off before she got a word out.

"My daughter, Edith, is currently staying with her aunt in Sussex. The length of her stay is uncertain. You see, Miss Bingley, just last week, Edith did what you are doing now. She spoke about Mrs. Darcy in a negative manner. She mocked her, spread tales about her, and even confronted her at a dinner party at our home. Mr. Darcy and Mr. Fitzwilliam Darcy caught her in the act, and their anger was fierce to behold. Indeed, Mr. Darcy nearly cut off the connection between himself and my family. The Darcys and Millers have been friends for decades, Miss Bingley. If Mr. Darcy was unafraid of cutting our connection, imagine how easy it would be for him to cut the connection between his family and yours, which is much newer. Mr. Fitzwilliam Darcy was as angry that night as I have ever seen him. If I did not know him so well, I would have been fearful of him striking my daughter. If she had been a man, I have no doubt he would have."

By this time, Caroline had rallied from her initial shock at being addressed so by a woman she barely knew and began to defend herself. "Mr. Darcy would never sever the connection between my brother and his son! Mr. Fitzwilliam Darcy is a grown man; his father cannot control who he be-friends. You are wrong to think such a thing! He and my brother are very close. Mr. Fitzwilliam Darcy would never turn his back on my brother over an insignificant baggage like Eliza!"

Miss Bingley had, by this time, worked herself into quite a rage. Her face was bright red and her hands were clenched into fists at her sides. She had managed to keep her voice lowered, but even that much control was becoming beyond her. She had one more thing to say to this interfering group of women, and then she intended to turn her back on them and exit the room, effectively cutting them. She opened her mouth to speak, but was cut off before she could begin.

Lady Matlock had listened to this young woman long enough. It was her niece this unimportant daughter of a tradesman was disparaging, and she would not stand for it. "Do you know who I am, Miss Bingley? I am the Countess of Matlock, a peer. I am also the aunt of Mrs. Darcy. Do you know what I could do to you socially? The misery I could inflict on your prospects? Think carefully, Miss Bingley, before you speak again. I will brook no disrespect towards my niece."

With this, the great lady moved away, followed one at a time by the rest of the group. Caroline Bingley, still violently angry, walked out of the room and up the stairs to her chambers. Peer or no peer, that woman had no business speaking to her as she did. None of them had. She wished her sister Louisa was here so she had someone to talk to about it. But no, Louisa had gone to Somerset to spend the holidays with her new husband's family. Angrily, Caroline paced her sitting room, back and forth and back and forth, until she heard sounds in the hallway indicating that the other guests were beginning to retire. She pulled the bell for her maid to attend her, not sure she was calm enough yet to sleep.

After she had a chance to expend some of her furious energy and think about the situation, she was calmer, but still angry. Yes, as a peer of the realm, Lady Matlock had power to ruin her standing in society. Yes, the daughter of one of those women had been sent away for maligning Eliza Darcy. That still did not give them the right to speak to her. She would not let them rule over her. She would be discrete, but she would not change her behavior.

<p style="text-align:center">~~~***~~~</p>

When the men joined the ladies after their port, Lord Walton immediately searched the room for Caroline. He was perplexed when he did not see her. He had been relieved to find in her an attractive woman with acceptable manners. Her dress was a little more extravagant than he was used to seeing and was a clear indication that she was "new money," from a family of tradesmen trying to move up in consequence. It was unfortunate, but it did not preclude her from consideration. In fact, from what he had seen so far, Miss Bingley would be a good choice. He moved to speak to her brother. I might as well get that part out of the way as soon as possible, he thought.

While Lord Walton was seeking out Mr. Bingley, Lady Matlock had seen her husband enter and moved across the room to intercept him. She wanted to let him know to warn George and Fitzwilliam about Caroline. This she accomplished quickly, returning to Elizabeth's side.

Lord Matlock, on the other hand, immediately strode to where Fitzwilliam stood with Bingley and Lord Walton. He caught his brother's eye as he moved, gesturing him to join them. "Gentlemen, we have something to discuss. Bingley, this involves you and your sister."

"Oh, well, in that case, given what Lord Walton and I have just now been discussing, perhaps he should hear it, as well. Lord Walton has asked permission to speak to Caroline alone in the morning. He wishes to marry her."

Lord Matlock sighed. "That might make this situation better, then. You are welcome to stay, Walton." Looking back at Bingley, he stated, "My wife just informed me that your sister has been slandering Elizabeth and treating her in an infamous manner. Lady Matlock and some of the other ladies spoke to her, urging her to change her behavior and citing a recent incident involving one of their daughters as evidence of what she might suffer if she continues. My wife reports that Miss Bingley responded in anger, and does not believe that your sister plans to make any changes but intends to continue in a like manner."

Here Fitzwilliam interjected his opinion. "Bingley, you are my closest friend, but I cannot allow that behavior toward my wife. Something must be done."

Bingley was embarrassed. How could Caroline do something like this? What was she thinking? She knew better than to behave in such a manner! What had happened to his sweet twin? He was going to have to speak to her as soon as possible, but for now, he needed to smooth things over with Darcy. He was not at all willing to risk his oldest and dearest friendship for his sister's desire to denigrate a perceived rival.

"I apologize, Darcy, Mr. Darcy, Lord Matlock. She had no right to do such a thing." Bingley looked at each man as he spoke, nodding at them and silently asking forgiveness. He could strangle his sister for putting him in this humiliating situation. "Lord Walton already asked permission to speak with her. Sir, how interested are you? Does it matter if she comes to you willingly? I can tell her that she has no choice, especially if she continues to behave so towards Mrs. Darcy. She has repeatedly and vehemently told me that she does not plan or desire to marry for love. She wishes higher connections and status. I doubt she would object to your person; though, she likely will object strenuously to being forced to do something. She likes to be in charge."

"I am very interested. It matters not to me how willing she is. It is helpful to my cause that she wishes to gain higher connections; she will be much quicker to agree. I can guarantee, Darcy, that she will not be put into a position again where she can slander or abuse Mrs. Darcy."

"Then it is settled," stated the elder Mr. Darcy. "Please let us know if there is any way we can help to move things along."

"We will, sir," replied Bingley, nodding to Lord Walton.

By this time, the ladies were done exhibiting and couples were beginning to wander up the stairs to their rooms. The gentlemen returned to their sides, escorting them to their rest for the night.

Upon him and his wife reaching their rooms and meeting in their bed to hold each other and talk, Fitzwilliam explained the arrangement between Lord Walton and Bingley.

"So, Miss Bingley is being forced to marry Lord Walton. I wonder how she will feel about being betrothed to someone she barely knows."

"Once she realizes his station in life, I am quite sure she will quickly resign herself to it. To be honest, a baron is far above what she could have reasonably expected."

"And he wants her just for her fortune? How sad. Is there nothing else he admires?"

"I know not, but you must admit she is a handsome woman. Not to me, of course," he quickly added as he lurched out of range of his wife's pinching fingers. Capturing her hand, he contin-ued. "If she did not present herself as so superior to the remainder of the world, she would likely have had other suitors before now. Perhaps she would even be married."

"She was holding out for you."

"She would have been waiting a very long time." He kissed her softly, his tongue caressing hers briefly before he slowly drew away. "I would have sooner or later offered for you. Your situation rushed things, but you were always in the back of my mind, even on my tour of the Kingdom. Every sight brought things to mind to share with you. You have always been a good friend." His eyes searched her glittering ones. "We were meant to be together."

She reached up to pull his head down for a kiss, and soon they were lost in each other once again.

Chapter 14

Bingley awoke the next day determined to speak to his twin as soon as possible. He asked his valet to inquire of Caroline's maid if she was awake and ready for visitors.

"Oh, and Bailey, if my sister is not going to be available to speak to me right away, ask her maid to tell her that I require an audience with her this morning, before she breaks her fast."

The manservant nodded and moved away to do his master's bidding. Within a few minutes, he returned with news that Miss Bingley would see her brother in her sitting room in a half-hour.

Bingley spent that time rehearsing what he would say. Caroline's actions were serious. Very serious. He did not know what was going on in her head to make her think such behavior as she had exhibited towards Mrs. Darcy most of this visit was acceptable. She did not normally behave in such a fashion, at least not when he was near. Certainly, when they were children she had been sweet-natured, much as he himself still was. However, when she had come back from school, he had noticed that something was a little different in her manner. Since it had never previously affected him directly, he had not thought much on it. Now he wished he had. He was not about to risk his relationship with his oldest and best friend to protect his most difficult sibling. Twins they might be, but the two were as different as night was from day at this point. He loved her dearly, but it was beyond time that she took responsibility for her actions.

When the appointed hour came, Bingley presented himself at his sister's sitting room door, knocking firmly. He gathered his fortitude around him like a great blanket as he waited for permission to enter. He was going to need as much of it as he could muster to get himself through this interview. Upon hearing Caroline's voice bidding him to enter, he took a deep breath and opened the door.

"Good morning Caroline," he began.

"Good morning, Charles. I was surprised at your summons so early in the day. Could this not have waited until after I had eaten?" Miss Bingley knew why her brother was standing before her. She hoped, however, to put him off. It was not that she thought she could manipulate him; he had always had the ability to stand up to her, or anyone who he felt was wrong. It was just that she knew how ladies in society were expected to behave, and Charles did not. He had not been to her school and learned what she had about moving amongst the higher classes. If the Bingley family were to join the highest circles, she must learn to behave appropriately. Nothing she had done this visit had been any different than what had happened in any other location where women gathered.

"No, Caroline, it could not. Would that I did not have to address it with you at all, but I must. I will not allow you to come between me and the man I count closer than a brother. Your behavior to Mrs. Darcy was beyond the pale. What has come over you to conduct yourself in such a way? You have never been vindictive before. And what about fawning all over Darcy? What were you thinking? Caroline, he is married. That is forever. He is out of your reach, not that he ever would have considered you in the first place. Not the way you have acted since you left school. What happened to change you?" By now, Bingley had grown angry. His face red, his arms waving, his pointing finger punctuated each point he made. Every time he looked at his twin, his fury grew, for she sat there as though she had not a care in the world. She looked bored, and if he had not been taught to never strike a lady, he would knock her off that settee and make her sit up and take notice. Instead he paused, turning away to look out the window and get his pique under regulation. No wonder Darcy does this so often, he thought.

"I did nothing wrong, Charles. Women of the ton speak in that manner to each other. It is the way things are done. I fail to understand why you are so upset."

Charles whipped around from the window to stare at her incredulously. "The way things are done? I have attended dozens of dinners, balls, and card parties, Caroline. I have observed Darcy's family … all of them, male and female alike … and have not seen them behave in such a manner, ever. I have been to St James' and Almack's and have never observed such goings on in either place. In public, Caroline, ladies do not behave in that way. What is appropriate in one's own home is completely different than what is allowed outside of it. I am not saying the gossiping you do in private is good, either, but it is definitely not acceptable elsewhere. Visiting a friend's home is the same as visiting in public when the gathering is this large and mixed with both family and those who are not. If you wish to defame anyone, not just Mrs. Darcy, do not do it in public! You are setting both of us up for failure, Sister, and I will not have it. Darcy is my oldest and dearest friend, and I will not lose that for anyone, not even you." Here Charles paused a moment to collect his thoughts.

"There are consequences and ramifications for every action a person takes. There are penalties which I must now enforce upon you so our family may maintain its respectability and retain the friendship of the Darcys. Again I say, Fitzwilliam is the brother I never had, and I will not give that friendship up. You have been acting strangely at times, ever since you returned from school. I have ignored it up until now, but no longer. Lord Walton had asked permission to speak to you about a courtship. However, he no more than made his request than Darcy's uncle informed me of your behavior, and Darcy himself told me in no uncertain terms that if it does not change, he will cut off our friendship. Walton was present during this discussion, and we decided that instead of courting you, he will marry you." Bingley raised his hand to quiet his sister, who had begun to speak out in protest. "Nothing you say matters at this point, Caroline. There is no other option for you. I will not have you in my household, and you know Hurst will not, either. It is beyond time that you married. You have been 'out' for four seasons. I know that you were holding out for Darcy, but that ship has sailed. You will be Lady Walton in a few weeks and that is that. He will speak to you later today, and you will accept him."

Caroline wilted a bit under her brother's glare. He was rarely as angry as he was at this moment. It was rather frightening to see, and she could not immediately think of anything to say to appease him. She did not, however, want to be told who she was going to marry. Why should she be forced to wed because she told some home truths about a meaningless country nothing? So she married Fitzwilliam Darcy … she was still a nobody. Tasteless, uncouth, and without manners. Still, another peek at Charles' face was enough to keep her from voicing those thoughts. *I had best try to calm him,* she thought.

"Very well, Brother. I will marry this Lord Walton." *Good, he seems to be relaxing a bit.* "I do not like being forced to wed, but to make you happy, I will," she sniffed, raising her chin. *Though that does not mean I will make it easy on Lord Walton.*

"Watch yourself, Sister; you do not want to trip because you cannot see past that nose you just stuck in the air. I do not want to hear a word out of you today beyond pleasantries. You will stay away from Mrs. Darcy. Do you understand me?"

"Charles, do not be ridiculous. How can I give Lord Walton an answer if I am not allowed to speak?"

"Caroline!" Bingley spoke sharply. "Do not give

me cause to add further punishments to you. You are in a dangerous situation for one of our standing. And do not think you are going to be difficult with Lord Walton about accepting him. I have already given him leave to affect a compromise, if needed. It does not matter to me how he goes about it. He can carry you off to Gretna Green for all I care. You will marry him, sooner rather than later." With that, Bingley marched out of his twin's sitting room, firmly shutting the door behind him.

His sister sat looking after him, mouth hanging open, shock clearly written on her face. He obviously was serious. She needed to be very careful for the next few days if she wanted to avoid any more of his censure. She knew, though, that she could be subtle. She need not change a thing, only appear to have.

Caroline truly saw nothing wrong with her behavior. Charles was correct – she had been out in society for four years. Before that, she had been at school for five years, rubbing shoulders with the daughters of families of the wealthy. A few were peers, but more were from families that ranged from new money like Caroline herself to ancient families with old money and high standing in society. Caroline had felt out of place when she first arrived. Her mother had instructed her to befriend those of elevated status and not waste her time with those of her social class. Her parent had made it clear to her and her sister that they were to raise the family's consequence through marriage and that she should make the most of every connection she could while at school.

So, when she had arrived at school and realized that maintaining the sweet personality she had grown up with was not going to help her but rather hinder her, she began to imitate those with whom she wanted to associate. It did not take her long to learn how to manipulate people, gossip about them, and put on airs. She achieved her goal – she was accepted into the highest circles of girls. Unfortunately, Caroline never learned the difference between behavior at school and behavior in public, in society. What one does to survive in a school setting does not translate into what is acceptable in the world outside. Caroline was stuck in behaviors learned years ago and could not see where she was wrong. Now she was paying a price.

When she finally came down for breakfast, Miss Bingley was subdued. Under the eagle eye of her brother, she politely greeted everyone in the room before settling down in the only available seat. As she began eating, she realized that to her right sat Lord Walton. She remained quiet; it was up to him to make the first move.

While she ate, she thought about the coming proposal. Though she hated having her choice taken away from her, in reality that had already happened when Fitzwilliam Darcy married. Why he chose to marry someone so beneath him was a mystery to her, but it was done and could not be undone. She turned her thoughts to Lord Walton. He was not a bad-looking man. If one were to be forced to marry against one's inclinations, one could do much worse. And, he was a peer. That would make her a peeress upon her marriage, which would give her a higher precedence than Mrs. Darcy. Happy thought! She could, and would, make sure to emphasize that as often as she could. After all, even a peer could be manipulated, and as a peeress she would be above censure. Miss Bingley smiled to herself as she finished her breakfast. Before she could rise from her seat, Lord Walton asked for a private audience with her. Smiling smugly, she agreed, and preceded him from the room.

~~~***~~~

The morning of the ball dawned bright and clear. There had been a brief snowstorm and lots of clouds the previous day. This morning, however, there was neither a cloud in the sky nor a flake in the air. The reflection of the sun off the beautiful covered-in-white landscape lifted the spirits of Pemberley's mistress after the tension of the last day or two. It helped to know that the dance would go on as planned, with no unexpected delays, as the snowfall had been minimal and not deep enough to delay travel.

Elizabeth walked with Mrs. Reynolds through the ballroom and dining room, checking the decorations and arrangements. The footmen and maids had gone out before the storm and gathered
~~~

enough greenery to fill the stillroom. Yesterday, they had spent all day turning it into garlands and other decorations, and hanging them all over the house. The ballroom was exquisite. Elizabeth was sure she had never seen such a well-decorated room in all her life. She knew the attendees at the ball would all remark on it.

The rest of the house was just as beautiful. There were garlands of holly and ivy draped over the banisters of the grand staircase and the doorways. The Yule log was in place in the sitting room fireplace. The kissing bough was delightful, and hung over the mantle of the same sitting room. Bunches of mistletoe hung over tables and other furniture in all the rooms. Both items, mistletoe and kissing bough, had already invited many pecks on the cheek amongst the staff, along with blushes and laughter. Even Mr. and Mrs. Reynolds had made use of both, to the delight of all who chanced to witness it.

Elizabeth felt a deep peace at such a beautiful setting for the first ball she had ever hosted. She knew deep inside that this was going to be a beautiful day, the beginning of a beautiful season. She had no fear of being insulted or despised. She was certain that her family had made sure all the guests knew she was to be respected. She loved Christmas and all it represented, and to be in such a wonderful position at this very special time of year gave a boost to her confidence and her emotions.

Her inspection complete, Elizabeth took her daily stroll around the upstairs hallways before breaking her fast with her guests and family. Fitzwilliam kissed her hand as she entered, escorting her to her seat next to him before moving to the sideboard to fix her a plate.

"Good morning, everyone," she greeted as she

sat down. Already at the table were Papa George, Mr. Bingley, and the Miller and Burns families.

"Good morning, Daughter," replied Mr. Darcy with a smile. "I trust you slept well? I heard you about with Mrs. Reynolds this morning. Is everything in order for tonight's entertainment?"

"Yes, sir; everything is perfect. All we need now are guests and musicians." Elizabeth smiled brightly at her father-in-law as she spoke, and then again at her husband when he set her plate before her and sat down next to her, reaching for her hand to squeeze.

"I expected no less, my dear. You have quite a talent for organization, and partnered with our housekeeper, you make a powerful team. This ball will be spoken of for years in the county, I am sure." Mr. Darcy beamed at his beautiful daughter-in-law, thinking once again that he was so very blessed to have her as part of his family.

After receiving the greetings and compliments of the rest of the occupants of the breakfast room, Elizabeth quietly ate her meal. She was very much distracted by her Fitzwilliam's presence and found herself staring at him frequently. She wished she could hold his hand while she ate, but that was impractical. She contented herself with watching him converse, sometimes with others but often with her. She loved his smile and the soft look in his eyes when he gazed at her. She hoped that they would have some quiet time together before she had to begin to bathe and dress for the ball.

After eating, the Darcys scattered to take care of some house- and estate-related issues while the rest of the party amused themselves for a couple of hours with cards or billiards or needlework. Soon they began drifting up the stairs to their rooms to begin getting ready for the night's entertainment.

Fitzwilliam had, upon escorting his wife from the breakfast parlor, whispered in her ear a suggested assignation for an hour hence. Elizabeth had agreed with a quiet giggle and now the two were upstairs in their suite seated together in the chair. He loved holding her this way, in his lap with her arms about his neck. It was his favorite way of spending time with the dearest person in his life. They chatted for a bit, punctuating their discussion with kisses that before long were increasing in length and intensity. His beloved wife was certainly amorous today, and Fitzwilliam was not about to stand in the way of her satisfaction. Soon the couple moved to the bed, forgetting about balls and baths and guests.

The pair was awakened by Elizabeth's maid, who had come to inform her mistress that her bath water was ready. Kissing each other softly, they parted ways, each to their own dressing room. They regretted that their private time was over for the time being, but they did have guests and a ball to host.

Later, as she sat at her dressing table while her maid finished putting up her hair, Elizabeth heard her spouse's soft knock on the door and bid him enter. As he moved into the room with a smile on his face, that special one that she knew was just for her, her heart beat faster. He was dressed in his black suit, with trousers instead of breeches, and a waistcoat that matched her dress. As a matter of fact, it looked to be of the same material and pattern. She still, after months of marriage, was not sure how that happened, as she was well-acquainted with the amount of material required to make a dress as well as the amount she had ordered. Someone somewhere must add extra fabric to each order she made. Regardless, he was looking rather dashing, and she greatly approved.

So busy was Elizabeth in admiring Fitzwilliam's figure, she did not see that he held something in his hand. Over the course of their marriage, he had several times given her a gift from the Darcy jewels. He approached her, reaching for her hand but urging her to stay seated at the dressing table. Leaning down, he kissed first her lips, then her ear, and finally her neck. As he was distracting her with those caresses, he brought a necklace around with his other hand and fastened it. It was a beautiful set of emeralds in a gold setting. Opening her eyes as she felt the ornament settle around her neck, she was struck by the beauty of them.

"Oh, Fitzwilliam! They are exquisite! Were they your mother's?" Elizabeth never knew if the gift he gave her on any particular day had been worn by his mother previously, or one of his other ancestors. He had even, on occasion, bought her jewels of her own. No matter the source, she appreciated each and every gift. The honor of wearing his mother's jewels was not lost on her, though. Those particular gifts reinforced in her mind that she was Mrs. Darcy, and she was highly esteemed. She would have loved him had he nothing to his name, of course, but those particular indications of his regard were valued the most.

"Yes, my darling, they were. I remember her wearing these to a Christmas ball the year before she passed. I wanted to present them to you today as a token of how proud I am of you and how you present yourself to everyone around you. You represent the Darcy family well, and I love you with all my heart."

Elizabeth rose from the bench to give him a hug and a kiss of thanks. She melted into him as he held her tightly to his chest. After a too-short hug, Fitzwilliam pulled back a bit, reaching into his pocket. "There are earrings and a bracelet to go with it, my love. Here, let me help you put them on, then we can go and begin to greet our guests."

With those words, he clasped the bracelet over her arm and attached the earrings to her lobes, then softly kissed her and led her from the room and down to the foyer to greet their guests.

In the entry hall, at the bottom of the grand staircase, Mr. Darcy stood watching his son and daughter descend. They made a fine-looking couple, and he was exceedingly proud of both of them. He was looking forward to the day he could dandle a grandchild on his knee, and he had a feeling that it would not be long before that happened. He had watched for months as the two fell deeper in love and had noticed that some days, today for instance, they could hardly keep their hands off each other. Yes, one day soon he would be a grandfather. He could hardly wait!

The Shetlers were the first of the guests to arrive. Not part of the house party, they had neverthe-less been to Pemberley for dinner a couple times in the last few days and had spent yesterday vis-iting Elizabeth and partaking in the amusements. First Mrs. Shetler and then Miss Shetler had squeezed Elizabeth's hands upon greeting her. She knew they would stand beside her come what may tonight, though truly, she had the feel-ing that everything would go smoothly. She knew without a doubt there would be no trouble from anyone tonight in regards to herself and her mar-riage. This was going to be a glorious night.

Once the last of the guests had been greeted and the Darcys entered the ballroom, Elizabeth's excitement was palpable. It had been months since she last danced with her husband, and they were participating in the first set. As they stood across from each other in the line, they gazed one at the other with looks of pure adoration on their faces. Those who were not dancing and prone to examination of those around them took note. Of course, the couple had been seen at events before now both in Derbyshire and in London, but they looked even more besotted with each other now than they had been just a week ago at the Millers' dinner.

Elizabeth and Fitzwilliam were blissfully unaware of the talk floating around them. When the music began and they took their first steps, it was as if the rest of the room ceased to be, and they were the only two people that existed. Their movements as they flowed through the steps were perfectly matched. Both exuded elegance and grace. They were two halves of a whole, mirrors of each other in movement, ability, and beauty.

Watching the couple from up the line were Miss Bingley and Lord Walton, whose engagement had been announced at dinner last night. This was their first appearance as a betrothed couple. Lord Walton saw the look on Miss Bingley's face as she watched the Darcys dance and felt it incumbent upon himself to warn her once again of the consequences should she cause trouble. As soon as the steps of the dance brought them close to each other, he leaned down and quietly said, "Remember what I told you, Caroline. There will be no trouble from you towards Mrs. Darcy, or we will be on the road to Gretna Green before the ball is over, and you will not get the big society wedding you want."

Miss Bingley startled from her contemplation of the couple down the line and turned her eyes to her betrothed. When she had agreed to marry him yesterday morning, he had warned her in no uncertain terms that her dream wedding and the amount of her future pin money depended upon her good behavior. She could choose to treat Mrs. Darcy poorly again, but she would find herself marrying in Gretna Green without her family and all of society witnessing her triumph. Or, she could behave with decorum and have the large wedding she desired. Walton had taken the time to outline for her the behavior he expected, in detail. She had tried to tell him that he could not possibly know how ladies behaved when gentlemen were not in the room, but he quickly reminded her of her roots and that she could not be expected to know that what happens at school stays at school. She was offended, of course, but

not enough to try to break off the engagement.
So, she agreed to amend her behavior for the
duration of the house party and into the future.
For, as she was informed, she would have a set
amount of pin money that good behavior would
add to. Bad behavior, however, would cause said
amount of pin money to diminish.

Caroline had at first tried to manipulate Lord
Walton into letting her have her way, but quickly
came to understand that he was not having it.
He made it plain that this was a marriage of
convenience, and that where it went from here
depended entirely upon her. He felt that they
could have a good relationship, if she behaved
appropriately. She was, however, from trade,
and so needed to be taught how to move about
in his circles. Miss Bingley was offended once
more, but again not enough to attempt getting
out of their arrangement. In the back of her

mind, his forcefulness actually intrigued her. No one had been that commanding with her, ever, except her brother when he confronted her that morning. She was curious about this feeling Lord Walton engendered in her and looked forward to learning more.

Therefore, when she heard his warning, she simply nodded her head in acknowledgement and continued dancing. She turned her head away from the direction of the young Darcy couple and focused instead on the man she was marrying.

After their set of dances ended, Fitzwilliam and Elizabeth began circulating around the ballroom, chatting with friends, making sure everyone was comfortable, and making introductions where necessary. At some point, Fitzwilliam had to leave her side to attend to his father and Elizabeth found herself surrounded by friends. To her left were the

Shetler ladies, and to her right was Lady Susan. The women had decided amongst themselves to guard the mistress of Pemberley and let it be known that she was not without friends. It was an unusual alliance, to be sure, since Lady Susan was of higher status and the Shetler ladies were not ones with whom she would usually align herself, but she had seen from their greetings that they were friends of Mrs. Darcy and therefore, she would be friends to them. She planned to make sure that there would be no further incidents like the ones with her daughter and Miss Bingley.

At the end of the night, the Darcys were congratulated on their fine event by all the attendees. They retired to their rooms, satisfied that their guests had enjoyed themselves and happy that there had been nothing untoward said or done in regards to Elizabeth and her marriage to her Fitzwilliam.

~~~***~~~

The next day was Christmas Day. As it was also the day after the ball, everyone at Pemberley was slow to rise. Breakfast had been planned for after church for that reason; however, the cook had decided to send small baskets of muffins along in the carriages in case anyone felt they needed something to tide them over.

Church was a special time for the Darcys and many of their guests. The Darcys in particular valued this time spent in God's house, praising Him and learning about Him. They had their own personal times spent in prayer and study at home every day, and Elizabeth and Fitzwilliam had time as a couple that they spent similarly, but going to church and participating in corporate prayer and fellowship was important to them. On this day, the day they celebrated the birth of the Savior, they were even more rever-
~~~

ent than usual. All were thankful for the acceptance last night of Mrs. Darcy by the guests in attendance and prayed with extra gratitude. That gratitude magnified the entire service for many in attendance. The music seemed sweeter, the sermon seemed more personal, and the prayer seemed more meaningful.

After the moving service, the Darcys and their guests returned to the manor house for a warm breakfast and more camaraderie. The visitors would all be leaving tomorrow morning, going back to their own homes to celebrate Twelfth Night, so they spent the day enjoying each other's company and relaxing.

Just before luncheon, Mr. Darcy asked Georgiana, Fitzwilliam, and Elizabeth to meet him in his private sitting room. The Darcy family, in opposition to most of the country at this time, had always practiced gift-giving, in a small way. Each member of the family gifted the others with a small token, sometimes a much-desired volume, sometimes a small box of a favored candy, or perhaps a pair of gloves. This day, with guests in the house, Mr. Darcy decided to go ahead with the exchange of gifts, but in the privacy of his chamber. To each of his children, Elizabeth included, he gave a book. Georgiana received a book of fairy tales, while his daughter-in-law and son each received a book of poetry. Expressing their delight, his daughters each gave him a hug. His son shook his hand, gripping it tightly.

Georgiana gave each of her siblings and her father a handkerchief embroidered with their initials. She was learning needlework, and was eager to show off that accomplishment. She was exclaimed over by all the adults and given tight hugs and many compliments.

The married Darcy couple gave gifts to Georgiana and Papa George, but saved their gifts to each other for later in the evening after they retired for the night. Mr. Darcy received a new pair of riding gloves, and Georgiana a set of watercolors. Each gift was gratefully received.

Later that night, before they went to bed, Elizabeth and her beloved Fitzwilliam exchanged their gifts. They had each gotten the other a new journal. They laughed at this, as it showed how in-tune to each other they were. As they snuggled in tight to each other to sleep, both said a silent prayer of thankfulness for the love and the wonderful life they shared.

The next morning, they arose early to see their guests off. As the last carriage pulled away, they happily turned to the activities that pleased them most. Mr. Darcy retired to his study to take care of Pemberley business, Georgiana to the music room to practice, and Fitzwilliam and Elizabeth to the library to cuddle by the fire and read.

Chapter 15

The Darcy family enjoyed the winter at Pemberley, once the holiday festivities had played themselves out. At that time, the weather turned snowy. For weeks, no one stirred from before their fire except to tend to livestock. There was no riding about the estate, no visiting the neighbors or shopping in Lambton, and no going to church. Not even the post made it through the deep snowdrifts and bone-chilling cold. Eventually, however, the weather broke, becoming milder and giving the residents of the area a chance to dig themselves out and move about once more.

By the last day of January, the entire Darcy family had returned to town. Georgiana willingly went back to school, eager to share with her friends stories of her time away and to hear theirs. Her father and siblings were equally as willing, though perhaps less eager, to do their duty, as well.

For the adult Darcys, the season meant returning to the endless rounds of balls and parties. Fitzwilliam had never enjoyed socializing. He found it much easier to bear with a wife at his side. Elizabeth was not averse to it, really, but in the past year had suffered greatly at such events. However, she was returning to town this time with a sense of confidence she had not felt for almost a year. She was determined to allow no one to intimidate her ever again. George Darcy had no strong feelings about the season at all. It was simply his duty to attend events and represent his family.

Jane joined them at Darcy House in mid-

February, after spending a few weeks with the Gardiners. Her courtship with Bingley was progressing well. She had missed his company while he was in Derbyshire, and was glad to see him when he returned. Now that she was staying with her sister, she knew she would see more of him and accompany him to as many events as possible. The only thing that would make her happier was an offer of marriage.

The Darcys had not been long returned before invitations began to pour in. Every day's post brought another handful. Most were discussed and the relative merits of attendance decided upon before a decision was made. Of course, some events were more important than others. A few were immediately consigned to the fire. Eventually, the most important first event of the season was deemed to be a ball to be held at St. James' Palace, in one week.

Generally, an event such as this would require a new gown. However, since Elizabeth had dresses that she had not yet worn, and styles had not changed significantly from last season, according to Madame Claire, she decided to wear something from her closet. Madame was relieved, for even though a rush order would mean more money in her pocket, there were many ladies who ordered at the last possible minute. Mrs. Darcy had commissioned an impressive amount of new gowns for the season; she was not concerned about the extra payment and appreciated having more time to work on other orders.

The day of the ball, Elizabeth prepared with a glint in her eye. Everyone around her from her servants to her family noticed something was different. She answered no inquiries, however. When her husband asked after her health, she simply assured him she was well. When her maid asked if there was anything she could get for her mistress' comfort, Elizabeth replied with a quiet, "No, thank you." When she finally descended the stairs to where Fitzwilliam and Papa George stood waiting, the stunned looks on their faces elicited a smug one on hers.

Mr. Darcy looked away, hiding the smile that had begun to spread at the dumbfounded look his son was giving Elizabeth. Given the self-satisfied one she wore, this was planned.

"Elizabeth," Fitzwilliam stuttered, "you look … magnificent!"

"Thank you, my love. Are we ready?" She inquired as he took her hand.

"Indeed. We were waiting only upon you." He paused before asking, "Are you well?"

"Yes, darling, I am very well. I cannot explain it,

but I feel somehow different. I know I will likely face continued criticism, but I survived last season's events, as well as those in Derbyshire this summer. I know I have your support and that of Papa George," She squeezed her husband's hand with her own while reaching her free one out to her father-in-law. Holding it tightly and looking up to his face, she continued. "Perhaps I have my confidence back in some measure. I know that besides having two such handsome defenders by my side, I am wearing a stunning gown that leaves me feeling beautiful whenever I look in the glass. Perhaps," she teased, "two gentlemen such as you do not understand the power of a good wardrobe."

Her husband and his father laughed, before letting her go so she could don the pelisse held by the maid. They entered the carriage in high spirits.

Hours later, they disembarked in the same mood. This first ball had been a wild success for Elizabeth. All of London society would be talking on the morrow of her poise and serenity. She had shown no fear, and even the Prince Regent had asked her to dance, entranced as he was with her display of assurance and wit.

Her triumph did not end there. At every event she attended, she gathered more admirers, both male and female. And with every admirer gained, her confidence grew. By the end of this season, her second as a married woman, Elizabeth Darcy would be known far and wide as a woman worthy of deference and respect. There were, as there always will be, naysayers; but her certainty that she belonged, combined with the sure knowledge of all the ton that her family members were her staunchest supporters, convinced the majority to accept her unconditionally. She was actively sought as a guest at every event, and her patronage requested for the most popular charities.

Her husband and her Papa George could not have been more proud. And while Fitzwilliam resented every dance that took her away from him and into the company of another man, he contented himself with the knowledge that it would be he taking her home. His wife encouraged him to dance rather than stand along the wall and glower at her partners, and to please her, he began asking the young ladies who lacked partners. His own reputation in society was raised as a result, for he was no longer seen as quite so haughty.

While their evenings were filled with enjoyable, though exhausting, soirees, the Darcys' days were less varied. As usual, George and his son were taken frequently with business. Often it was Pemberley business, but there were other estates to manage, as well as investments.

Elizabeth maintained in London the habit she had begun at home of beginning her day in conference with the housekeeper. Mrs. Bishop was very glad to see her mistress much recovered from the happenings of last year. She was in the habit of exchanging letters with Mrs. Reynolds, who could not say enough good things about Mrs. Darcy and her progress with all things related to a household. To see evidence of it before her was a glorious thing.

As often as they could, the Darcys visited with the Gardiners, either at Darcy House or at the Gardiner home. The family had been unable to visit this past summer, due to a new addition to the family. Mrs. Gardiner had been suffering from the early effects of a pregnancy at that time, and her spouse had decided to keep his wife at home. It was the first summer they had missed visiting the Darcy estate in many years, and the loss was keenly felt by all.

~~~***~~~

One of the activities that Elizabeth was required to participate in was visits. Her day "at home" was Wednesday, and her day every week for visiting was Thursday. Her feelings about these visits were mixed. While she felt as confident as ever, it did not follow that she desired to spend any more time with members of her new society than she absolutely had to. However, one could learn quite a bit if one kept one's lips closed and ears open during these visits.

One of the things she learned a month into the season was about her former nemesis, Lady Penelope Mays. When she later related the sto-
~~~

ry to Fitzwilliam, she was all glee, for despite doing her best to live in love with all men, as she learned in church, she was still a human being with all the frailties accompanying that state.

"Lady Susan was there, Fitzwilliam, and do you know what she told me?"

"No, but judging by the eagerness in your voice, it must have been very interesting."

"Indeed it is! She told me that she heard from Mrs. Jackson that Lady Penelope has disappeared."

"Disappeared! Is it certain?" By now, Fitzwilliam could see why Elizabeth was so excited by the news. He was certainly intrigued!

"Quite certain. Mrs. Jackson had it in a letter from a neighbor. You know, of course, that the Mays' estate is in the same area as the Jacksons'." At his nod, she added, "Well, this neighbor of the Jacksons added into this letter that Lady Penelope's maid was looking for a position, and when the maid was asked why she was let go, said that her mistress had packed a bag and rode away one night on a draft horse. No one saw Lady Penelope; the horse was missing in the morning and when it was discovered that the daughter of the house was also missing, it was assumed the two events were related."

"And there has been no word of her?"

"None."

"Did her father search for her?"

Elizabeth nodded, "According to Mrs. Jackson's information, yes. For months. I cannot imagine he has stopped as of yet. I certainly would never stop searching for my daughter, were she to go missing."

"I can guarantee that no daughter of ours would ever go missing. Any girls we have will be raised to respect themselves and others, including their parents," Fitzwilliam declared firmly. "But in the event one of your daughters should be so rebellious as to disappear in the night, be assured I would leave no stone unturned in the search to return her to you."

"Oh, she would be my daughter, were she to disappear?"

"Indeed," he replied in the haughtiest voice he could manage given his position in bed with his wife and the accompanying nudity. "For no daughter of mine would ever be inclined to leave my side. From you, however, they would run screaming as soon as they were of age!"

Elizabeth's mouth hung open for few seconds, partly in surprise at her husband's tease but partly because she had no words with which to fight such a fanciful notion.

"Well. Are we not just full of ourselves tonight? It would not be me they flee, oh husband mine, but you and your ever-present scowl." She scoffed, narrowing her eyes at his innocent look. "For that, you will pay," she added, attacking his sides with her fingers.

He yelped at the unexpected assault, curling into a ball, at the same time grabbing for one of her hands. Not too much later, he was the tickler and she his victim, until she pled for mercy and he let her go.

<div align="center">~~~***~~~</div>

One day not long after this conversation, Fitzwilliam and Elizabeth planned to go shopping. Fitzwilliam's favorite book shop had some new volumes recently delivered, and he wished to peruse them as soon as possible. They were to make other stops, as well, and so as they broke their fast that morning, they asked Mr. Darcy if he should like to ride along. He declined, citing a meeting with his attorney.

Shortly after his children left for Bond Street, Darcy also boarded a carriage. Four streets away, he realized he had forgotten a sheaf of papers he needed, and rapped on the carriage to alert the driver to stop. After a brief conversation between Darcy and a footman, the equipage moved again, this time turning down a side street to make the trip back to Darcy House.

Unbeknownst to Darcy, a young man he would have trusted with his life was about to steal from him. George Wickham, son of Pemberley's steward, was a favorite of George Darcy's, his godson, and he had provided in his will a living that would set the young man up for life, if he would take Holy Orders.

Young Wickham was outgoing and charming, the total opposite of Darcy's own son. The boys had practically grown up together at Pemberley, as close as brothers, or so Darcy thought.

Once he had sent the boys off to school, he began noticing a subtle change in their relationship. Attributing it to the expansion of their group of friends, he paid it no mind. However, upon the young men reaching University, the chasm between them seemed to grow wider. Fitzwilliam was unfailingly polite to his childhood playmate, but when it came time to socialize, he chose other companions. Darcy could not imagine them growing completely apart, so again he let it go, hoping that with time and maturity, they would mend fences.

Then one day last spring, shortly before Fitzwilliam's marriage, Darcy had learned, while dining at White's with another landowner, of many misdeeds that his favorite had committed. Not inclined at first to believe what he considered an idle report, he learned that his tablemate gained his information from his own son, who was part of the group that entered Cambridge when Fitzwilliam and young Wickham did. The next time Darcy saw his godson, he witnessed inappropriate behavior on Wickham's part towards Elizabeth and discerned Fitzwilliam's anger. He had given Wickham a stern talking to and sent him off with a few coins in his pocket, trusting that the boy would straighten himself out.

So, when he walked back into his study on this particular morning, he was shocked to see his favorite trying to pick the lock on a strongbox that held money for the household accounts.

"George! What are you doing?"

George Wickham jumped, as he had not heard the old man enter the room. "Um, I was just ..." He stammered. "Fitzwilliam asked me to bring some funds to him. He was ... he was at the confectioner's with Mrs. Darcy and forgot his wallet."

Darcy knew this information was incorrect, because he had spoken to his son and daughter-in-law not thirty minutes previously. They were not likely to rush through a visit to a bookshop, not even for sweets.

"I think not, son. Come." He gestured the young man around the desk to the settee in front of the fireplace. Reluctantly, Wickham did so. He was certain he would be able to talk himself out of his predicament, given enough time. Recalling his last conversation with his patron, he swallowed nervously. He was unsure just how much time it might take.

Unfortunately for Wickham, as he came around the desk, he caught his coat pocket on the corner, ripping it. Out onto the floor spilled a fortune in jewelry and other small, saleable items. Horrified, he looked at his godfather, and knew without the shadow of a doubt he would not be getting out of anything.

"What have we here?" Darcy asked. The disappointment in his voice could not be more clear. "Where did you get these items?" He paused, then. "I know this necklace. Fitzwilliam gave it to Elizabeth as a wedding gift. It was his mother's. You stole from my household!"

Wickham flinched at the stirrings of anger he heard in Darcy's voice. All his words to himself last spring about the unfairness of his situation as the poor son of a steward momentarily fled his memory. He had never before seen his godfather angry at one of his escapades. Disconcerted, he was silent for a few minutes, until he heard Darcy ask the butler to send for the constable.

He spent the next quarter hour justifying his actions, his resentments bubbling to the surface, but his words only solidified the hurt and anger of the older man. When he had expended his charm, explanations, and anger, he became silent.

"I favored you in part because your father is my most trusted employee, and because I could see something in you. You have the makings of a great man, if you would but apply yourself to some useful employment.

"Fitzwilliam is my son, and yes, he is my heir. I am sorry that by affording you the privileges I have, I caused you to become resentful of your situation and your station in life. I had never imagined such a thing. You have always been so charming and happy in appearance. I thought I was assisting you by welcoming you as I would a second son." Darcy's sadness and disappointment were clear in his voice.

He was silent for a few minutes as he contemplated his next step. "I told you what I expected of you. I will not bend in this, George," Darcy informed him. "After our chat a year ago, I thought you understood that your future rested on good behavior. How you count that as stealing from one as close as family to you, I do not understand."

After this, there was silence again, as Darcy composed a letter and recalled the butler to send it express. Turning back to Wickham, he began, "That was a letter for your father. I have requested his presence as soon as may be. I will not hide this from him, poor man. I can only imagine how much greater his disappointment with you will be."

"Yes, sir."

Before another word could be spoken, the constable arrived, and Darcy had Wickham carried off to Newgate. His last words to his godson, before the young man was led away, were, "Think about this, my boy. Think about the trust you were given, and that you betrayed. Think about the future you could have had and the future that could very well be yours now."

A week later, John Wickham was knocking on the door to Darcy House, the express from the master in his hand. His shame was great as he entered the study.

"I am so sorry, Mr. Darcy. I do not know what has got into him!"

"Rest easy, John. Come, sit with me, and we can discuss our options."

Ringing for tea, Darcy urged his steward into a seat on the settee, then took the armchair nearest to him. While they waited, Darcy explained the situation more fully. Wickham was mortified.

"I blame my late wife, sir. She was never happy with what I was able to provide. Once she was gone, I was better able to economize, and I tried to assure George that I was well able to afford an inheritance for him when I leave this earth, but her complaints must have had a greater impact than I thought," he sighed. "What have you done with him?"

"I sent him to Newgate, though I have provided sufficient funds for him to have clean bedding and clothing and good food."

"Thank you, sir. He does not deserve such consideration," Wickham responded bitterly.

"None of that, now. He is young and foolish, I agree, but there is hope for him yet."

"I hope so, sir." He paused before admitting, "I had heard rumors of his misbehavior but did not believe them at first. I trusted him so far as to not question him at all. Eventually, when enough tales of gambling and debauchery reached me, I began to see they must be true." He stopped for a moment to wipe at his eyes. "I feared for him, sir. Even as I prayed he would begin to accept his place in society, I was afraid something like this would happen. I should have spoken to him, remonstrated him. I have failed in my duty as a father, instead leaving it to you to teach him. I apologize."

Darcy hastened to reassure him. "I share in the

blame, as well. Fitzwilliam, I learned, has been covering George's misdeeds for years. He did not want me to be hurt. I noticed a strain between them, but instead of questioning the boys, I let it go." He shook his head. "If I could go back and begin again, I would have discussed what I saw with both of them."

The two men sat in contemplation for a brief time, until Wickham inquired about the theft. He dreaded the response but had to face it.

Darcy sighed before answering, "He had enough stolen items in his pockets to send him to the gallows."

Wickham gasped, covering his eyes with his hand to hide the tears that gathered there.

Seeing his steward's response, Darcy leaned forward, urging him not to despair. "Fear not; I believe I have a solution. If you are agreeable, he will not hang."

He went on to explain that, were it acceptable, Darcy would pay passage for George to Canada, with the proviso that he never return to England. Darcy was certain he could convince the judge to approve the punishment in lieu of any other. Wickham agreed, expressing his gratitude over and over to his employer.

"Say no more, John. You have been a faithful employee and companion these many years, and George is my godson. I could do no less."

"Thank you, sir. I will be off to Newgate now, to inform my son of what awaits him. I wish to do my utmost to impress upon him the opportunity he is being afforded, and the alternative that lay before him."

Shaking hands, the two men parted company.

~~~***~~~

Two weeks later, George Wickham boarded a ship bound for Canada. His interview with his father had been harsh, for his parent had given no quarter. No excuses were acceptable, no reasons rational. He had never in his life seen John Wickham so angry.

Despite the life of dissolution he had led the last few years, George was ashamed of himself for so distressing his only remaining parent. He had not considered anyone's feelings but his own; it had never occurred to him that, should word of his actions even reach Derbyshire, they would have an effect on anyone there.

His father and godfather were both at the dock to see him board the ship and sail away. Each man had taken the opportunity to admonish him to take advantage of this new life and turn him-
~~~

self around. He sighed to himself as he listened, nodding in all the right places. Being banished forever to the wilds of Canada did not sound like a pleasant opportunity to him. However, with the alternative being a noose around his neck, he had no other choice. He would go and make the best of it, but he refused to be happy.

~~~***~~~

Not long after the Darcys' return to town and plunge into the social whirl of the Season, Elizabeth began to sleep more than was normal. She thought little of it at first. After all, they were up for hours every night eating, drinking, and dancing, and when they retired, there were other activities that simply must be participated in before she and her husband were able to sleep. Who would not be more tired than usual after a couple weeks of constant activity?
~~~

Eventually, though, she began to notice other things that had changed. For example, her bosom was tender. She discounted amorous activities with Fitzwilliam as a cause of that. They had been married nigh onto a year. Surely any of that should have passed long ago.

Another strange thing was that she could no longer stand to be in the room with certain smells, for they made her nauseous. Cigar smoke was one of the worst, but at times, food smells caused a similar reaction.

When the day came that she lost the contents of her stomach upon arising, she knew she needed advice, for while she thought she knew what was wrong, she was not certain. Thankfully, Fitzwilliam had already arisen and was not in the bedroom. She shuddered to think of his reaction to such an event. After getting cleaned up and dressed, she dashed a quick note off to her Aunt Gardiner, asking her to come visit today, if she could make the time.

What her aunt had to say to her both frightened and delighted her. She was to be a mother! She asked what felt like a million questions, and her aunt patiently answered each.

"I shall have to tell Fitzwilliam! Oh, but wait …" She paused. "His mother died in childbirth. He told me she struggled through several miscarriages and they weakened her. I have seen his discomfort with pregnancies. How am I going to tell him?"

"Why do you not wait until you feel the babe move before you share this with him? Surely it will be soon; I estimate you are several weeks along, and they generally make themselves known to the mother when she is three months or so. Perhaps once you are past the most common period of miscarriage, he will not fret as much," she advised. "You will need to alert Mrs. Bishop. She will be very helpful to you, and I daresay she is able to keep a secret for a few weeks. Also, tell your maid. Then, call the doctor or a midwife to come examine you. Either of them will be able to reassure him of your fitness. Gaining information is likely the best way to keep him calm."

Nodding, Elizabeth replied, "I will do that. Thank you so much, Aunt Maddie!"

As Mrs. Gardiner stood to leave, the two embraced tightly. "I am so proud of you, Niece. I have heard of the wonderful impression you have made upon the ton since your return, and to see the sparkle in your eyes today and the self-assurance with which you carry yourself is a joy. My Lizzy is back, and I am delighted!"

"Thank you. I could not have done it without you and Uncle, nor without my husband and new family. I love you!" Kissing her aunt's cheek, she let her go.

Six weeks later, as she was dressing, Elizabeth felt a flutter in her belly. She stilled, waiting for it to happen again. When it occurred a second time, then a third, her smile of delight grew. She caressed over the spot where she now had proof that a baby rested – her baby with her wonderful, loving husband. She whispered to it, "Welcome, my darling child. Now I may tell your Papa about you."

As she turned to leave the room and find her husband, the door opened and in he walked. "Elizabeth," he began, "we have to talk. Come; sit here with me on the settee."

Alarmed, she sat where he indicated, asking,

"What is wrong? Is it Papa George? Should I go to him?"

"No, no, my love, nothing like that." He paused to gather his thoughts. He knew better than to just blurt them out. That always caused misunderstandings with his Elizabeth, and what he had to discuss was far too important to be disrupted by an argument.

"I want you to see a doctor." He held up his hand when her mouth opened. "I know you think you have hidden it, with the help of Jenny and Mrs. Bishop, but I have noticed your tiredness of late, not to mention that when we love each other, your moans are not always of ecstasy, and you are rushing off in the mornings to use the chamber pot … and I hear you being ill."

Now he stood and began pacing. "I have waited and waited for you to say something but you have not. I want a doctor to examine you so we can make sure there is nothing seriously wrong with you." He sat back down, grasping her hands in his. "I love you too much to lose you, Elizabeth."

She smiled at him, removing one hand from his and brushing hair away from his eyes, tenderly running her fingers down his cheek. "My love, I will agree to see the doctor if you will listen to me first. I have news for you."

At his nod, she continued. "Fitzwilliam ... I be-lieve we are to be parents this autumn."

Her husband sat there, staring. He was not en-tirely sure he understood. "Parents? We are to be parents?"

"Yes, silly." She laughed. "You are to be a father and I am to be a mother. I am with child."

His eyes bulged and his head came forward as his eyes dropped to her midsection and his mouth fell open. He gently laid his free hand over her stomach. "A child? Inside you?" He looked up at her, joy beginning to appear in his eyes. "My child! Inside you!" The more he thought about it, the more smug he got. "I did that," he declared with a wide grin.

"Yes, well, you did have a little help," his wife stated dryly as her eyes rolled.

Fitzwilliam jumped up, pulling her with him. "A baby! We must go tell Father!" He grabbed her hand, pulling her laughing from the room.

~~~***~~~

Mr. Darcy was thrilled to hear of his coming grandchild, and when the boy was born, crowed about it to everyone he knew. He spoiled the child, named George Bennet Fitzwilliam Darcy
~~~

but called Ben by his family, insisting on holding him as often as possible and giving in to his every cry. It was only by the sheer determination of his parents that as the child grew, he was sweet and gentle rather than haughty and demanding.

Ben was followed over the years by six siblings, two more boys and four girls. Pemberley and its residents were filled with love and laughter for many years.

~~~***~~~

Bingley proposed to Jane after a six-month courtship. They married from Longbourn, and leased Netherfield when its owner moved permanently to London. After a year and before the birth of their first child, they purchased an estate not thirty miles from Pemberley, to the delight of the sisters. The road between the estates was well-traveled.
~~~

Georgiana attended school until she was seventeen, at which time she was presented and survived her first season. When she was twenty, she fell madly in love with a viscount who was equally enamored of her. They married and had four children together. Fears that she was too much like her mother to survive childbirth were put to rest.

Lord Regis never bothered the Darcys again. He refused all invitations to balls and dinners, completely withdrawing from society. That summer, immediately following the death of his mother, he removed to one of his estates in Scotland, near Dumfries. There he met and married a local, very wealthy, gentleman's daughter, before even half of his mourning was over.

Elizabeth's relationship with her mother remained strained for the rest of that lady's life.

She was never invited to Pemberley, though her husband and other children were. Nor did Elizabeth ever again visit Longbourn. Mrs. Bennet never learned to recognize her misbehavior, instead blaming it all on Elizabeth, who, when her mother passed, mourned the relationship she didn't have more than the person who died.

Both Elizabeth and her adoring husband were happy to see her return to the confident lady she had been before their marriage, the one whose courage rose with every attempt to intimidate her. The gossips of the *ton* quickly moved on to fresh meat, and those ladies and gentlemen who remained antagonistic toward her were quickly conquered by her ready wit and sly insults. While still more careful about how she presented herself to people and less apt to trust quickly, she was no longer fearful. She was safe, had a husband who loved her to distraction, and the support of her extended family.

The End

Before you go …

If you enjoyed this book, please consider leaving a review at the store where you purchased it.

Also, consider joining my mailing list at

https://mailchi.mp/ee42ccbc6409/zoeburtonsignup

~Zoe

About the Author

Zoe Burton first fell in love with Jane Austen's books in 2010, after seeing the 2005 version of Pride and Prejudice on television. While making her purchases of Miss Austen's novels, she discovered Jane Austen Fan Fiction; soon after that she found websites full of JAFF. Her life has never been the same. She began writing her own stories when she ran out of new ones to read.

Zoe lives in a 100-plus-year-old house in the snow-belt of Ohio with her Boxer, Jasper. She is a former Special Education Teacher, and has a passion for romance in general, Pride and Prejudice in particular, and stock car racing.

Connect with Zoe Burton

Email:

zoe@zoeburton.com

Facebook:

https://www.facebook.com/ZoeBurtonBooks

https://www.facebook.com/groups/BurtonsBabes

Pinterest:

https://www.pinterest.com/zoeburtonauthor/

Website:

https://zoeburton.com

Join my mailing list:

https://mailchi.mp/ee42ccbc6409/zoeburtonsign
up

Support me at Patreon:

https://www.patreon.com/zoeburtonauthor

Me at Austen Authors:

http://austenauthors.net/zoe-burton/

More by Zoe Burton

Regency Single Titles:

I Promise To…

Lilacs & Lavender

Promises Kept

Bits of Ribbon and Lace

Decisions and Consequences

Mr. Darcy's Love

Darcy's Deal

The Essence of Love

Matches Made at Netherfield

Darcy's Perfect Present

Darcy's Surprise Betrothal

To Save Elizabeth

Darcy Overhears

Merry Christmas, Mr. Darcy!

Darcy's Secret Marriage

Darcy's Christmas Compromise

Darcy's Predicament

Darcy's Uneasy Betrothal

Darcy's Yuletide Wedding

Darcy's Unwanted Bride

Mr. Darcy: They Key to Her Heart

Darcy's Christmas Ball

Darcy's Christmas Scheme

Darcy's Favorite

Darcy's Happy Compromise

Victorian Romance:

A MUCH Later Meeting

Westerns:

Darcy's Bodie Mine

Bundles:

Darcy's Adventures

Forced to Wed

Promises

Mr. Darcy Finds Love (available exclusively to newsletter subscribers)

The Darcy Marriage Series Books 1-3

Mr. Darcy, My Hero

Coming Together

Christmas in Meryton

The Darcy Marriage Series:

Darcy's Wife Search

Lady Catherine Impedes

Caroline's Censure

Pride & Prejudice & Racecars

Darcy's Race to Love

Georgie's Redemption

Darcy's Caution

www.ingramcontent.com/pod-product-compliance
Lightning Source LLC
Chambersburg PA
CBHW050955210726
48287CB00004B/1230